WHAT GOES AROUND COMES AROUND

ACKNOWLEDGEMENTS
I would like to thank the following people for their input,
help and encouragement in completing this novel. For the great idea
and design of the cover my thanks go to John Revel, who is already
working on the cover for the follow up to *The English Sombrero*.
To Charlotte Stock for editing and proofreading. Mónica Bratt and
Anthony Duke for Art Direction and Artwork. My niece
Mandy Chivers who showed great a talent for deciphering my
scribbles and finally my sister and my wife who never lost faith in me.

Thank you and God bless.

Doug

GW00722348

There can be nothing more frustrating,
than a victim of a crime seeing the perpetrator
have no remorse.

Doug Goddard

WHAT GOES AROUND COMES AROUND

What would you do?

What would you have done?

Doug Goddard

First published in Great Britain in 2011
by Jemmett Affection Publishing
31 Hillview
Great Kimble
Buckinghamshire
HP17 9TR

A CIP catalogue record for this book is available from the British Library

ISBN 978 0 9552117 1 3

Produced by Anthony Duke Design

Art direction and coordination
Anthony Duke

Editor
Charlotte Stock

Printed and bound in Great Britain
by MPG Biddles Ltd

CHAPTER ONE

IT HAD BEEN THREE YEARS SINCE I HAD SEEN THAT FACE – a face that I could have poured acid over, a face I could have scored like a piece of pork, a drowning face I could have watched with ease fight for its last breath and do nothing. This was the face of Stephan Smith, the animal who raped my fifteen-year-old daughter and almost destroyed my whole family. He was now holding two fingers up to me and everything that is decent. This piece of shit had strutted back into my life via the front page of a daily tabloid.

The newspaper had devoted the whole page with headlines that read, "Lotto Lout Forces Neighbour Out." Time had not weathered or mellowed him: evil, arrogant and self-confident, his picture portrait said it all. Why now? Why had he come back? Flashes of that Saturday afternoon in February, when Hell visited our home shot through my head like a bolt of lightning. They were visions I had prayed never to see again.

The sound of the bells ringing from the medieval church snapped me out of my torment. Only after catching my breath and composing myself did I dare to look back at his picture. I stared into his eyes. How brave – me trying to outstare a picture from just a few feet away! Given the choice, would I rip it up or read it? Curiosity mixed with anger over the headlines began to run through me. Was it possible or even conceivable that scum like Smith would be allowed to hold on to so much money? My self-indulgent pity, which I had to hold deep inside, needed to be addressed. My wife and daughter were due to return from a shopping spree any moment and the likely consequences of them seeing Smith's face on the stranger's newspaper across the table would be torture of the worst kind for both Alison and Charlotte.

Our monthly shopping trip to La Bisbal over the past three years had become routine, and so had our time spent there. We would arrive about nine in the morning. Alison and Charlotte would head off shopping for two or three hours in the town and markets, while I amused myself browsing and occasionally buying items in my favourite ironmongers. Alison called it my Aladdin's cave. Afterwards I would sit and have a coffee on the terrace of Bar Hossa, weather permitting, in Church Square. The girls would join me there to enjoy one of Hossa's many excellent coffees before heading home, stopping on our way at our favourite restaurant in the village for the menu of the day. Otis, our son, would occasionally join us when he was able to grab a long weekend away from his duties at the main hospital in Barcelona.

Today, however, was different. I had asked the girls to return an hour early because I wanted to stop off to get the price on some chicken wire at the farming wholesalers, who always closed at midday on a Saturday. The church clock said five past eleven. I looked across the square towards the direction they would be coming from and to my horror they appeared right on time. It would be pointless changing tables. The bar only boasted six tables and we would be in view of that scum's face wherever we sat.

There was only one course of action open to me. I sprang out of my seat and towered over the stranger with the English paper.

"Excuse me."

The stranger lowered his paper and peered over his glasses at me. He was a man in his late fifties with a public school air about him.

"Good morning," he replied.

"Good morning," I said dutifully, "I need to ask a favour." There was no time for pleasantries, I needed to get straight to the point.

"Your newspaper – the picture on the front page is Stephan Smith. He raped my daughter three years ago. Both my wife and daughter are about to join me and if they catch sight of his picture it could prove devastating for us all."

"Dad, Dad!"

Charlotte had run ahead in front.

"Dad, Mum's seen a dress. You know that shop, the one you call the hippy shop?"

Charlotte was wildly excited – nothing unexpected where clothes were concerned.

"They're having a closing down sale because they're moving up the road, and everything's half price or less."

Alison arrived and dropped two heaving bags down beside her. Charlotte had managed to carry two bags but, as any mother knows, a mother will always carry the heaviest burden.

The stranger had now stood up. I quickly glanced down at the table and to my utter joy a picture of David Beckham stared back at me. The stranger had closed his paper then folded it only revealing half of the back page of sport. Charlotte was so excited and focused on getting me to part with money that she was oblivious to the stranger's presence; Alison meanwhile had made eye contact, I offered him an appreciative smile.

"Reginald Challenger. Just been saying to your husband what a lovely day it is." The stranger had gripped first Alison's and then Charlotte's hands in a firm handshake.

Yes, autumn's my favourite season," agreed Alison. "Are you on holiday, Mr Challenger?"

"No, I am fortunate to have the pleasure of living in this lovely part of the world at a place called Angies."

"It's about 10 to 15 miles north of Gerona."

I nodded that I knew of Angies. "My wife and daughter have a passion for buying clothes which borders on obsessive, Mr Challenger."

"Please call me Reg," he interrupted.

"I am just pleased they are both the same size, otherwise I would be bankrupt by now."

"Don't take any notice of my husband," protested Alison. I could see that Charlotte was about to chip in about how I would be saving money, so I caved in and handed over 300 euro.

"Go on, treat yourselves."

Charlotte landed a great big kiss on my cheek. "Thanks Dad."

"What about the chicken wire prices, Paul?" Alison asked.

I told her not to worry as it was going to be roughly the same price everywhere.

Suddenly a strong breeze swept from nowhere through the square. Parasols and trees that had stood motionless in the bright autumn morning suddenly came alive. The fierce gust of wind disappeared as fast as it had arrived, leaving in its wake just one disaster. Reg's newspaper managed to unfold itself and revealed

Stephan Smith's face once more. Seeing what had happened, Reg scooped up the paper quickly, folded it in half, and placed it on a chair under his other papers. Alison and Charlotte had not suspected anything thanks to Reg's quick reaction.

"Our English newspapers – 20 pages of adverts, 20 pages of rubbish and 20 pages of sport," he muttered.

"Nothing changes then," laughed Alison.

With his witty off-the-cuff remark Reg had averted a crisis for the second time today.

"Come on Mum," urged Charlotte, "Let's go!"

"We'll only be half an hour, love," promised Alison. She kissed me on the cheek then linked arms with her daughter and best friend as they walked back across the square like a couple of naughty schoolgirls who had just got away with some harmless mischief.

"Half an hour, a purse full of money and two women clothes-shopping, I should double that," I joked.

"You're one hundred percent right there," laughed Reg.

We both watched as the girls disappeared down the road to the right of the church. The warm contentment I felt whenever I saw those two so happy was beyond measure and a far cry from what could have happened if the stranger opposite me had not been so cooperative.

Reginald placed his papers back on the table. I glanced down at them and then looked up at him.

"Thank you."

"Close shave old boy."

"Yes," I agreed.

For a few seconds neither of us spoke.

"I'm about to order another coffee, care to join me?" inquired Reg.

"Thankyou but allow me to pay," I insisted.

We both sat down.

"Paul Taylor." I stretched across the table and we offered handshakes.

"Reginald Challenger, but I prefer Reg," he replied.

For a few minutes we exchanged pleasantries about where we lived, the football match we'd both watched the previous evening between Barcelona and Arsenal and, of course, the weather. Despite this, my mind continued to focus on the newspaper. Its contents kept goading me. Curiosity was getting the better of me but asking Reg if I could look at his paper would be like betraying my family's trust.

When we moved to Spain three years ago we decided to integrate one hundred percent, both in the community and the country. As a result, English newspapers and TV were the first things to go. Translating and struggling to make ourselves understood wasn't easy at times. Both the language and the culture were a challenge but after only a few months things started to become second nature to us. But now, not knowing what the newspaper said was going to torment me. I convinced myself that my family would never know what I was about to do. That made it okay.

Reg was more than happy to comply and handed over to me the paper with Stephan Smith's face on it. While Reg busied himself with another tabloid, I studied the photos on the front page. Next to Smith's portrait was an aerial view of his eight-bedroom mansion and surrounding land, which dwarfed a neighbouring modest three-bedroom bungalow. An inset picture showed a frail old couple, Mr and Mrs Williams. Compelled to find out the connection, I took up the invitation to 'Turn to page 5 for the full story'. Under the headline, 'The police are powerless', the article revealed that after scooping £56 million on the Eurolottery two years ago, Stephan Smith had bought the mansion and lived there with his mother, stepfather, two brothers and two cousins. Over the past two years, the police had been called in more than twenty times in response to incidents involving the Smiths and their neighbours the Williams, but to date no charges had been brought. The Williams had both been found dead in their home. No suspicious circumstances, but for their daughter it was clear who was to blame for their rapid and miserable demise.

The couple's daughter, Mrs Janet Hoddley, said her parents' health had deteriorated since Smith's arrival at the mansion and their lives had been made a misery by the intolerable noises, smells and constant abuse that came from their neighbours on an almost daily basis. Smith did not farm his land, but made a point of regularly spreading muck over the land that surrounded their bungalow. The stench made it impossible for them to go in their own garden or to have their windows open. The daughter declared that her parents had effectively become prisoners in their own home. Confrontations had arisen on the single track lane that ran past both properties, with Smith refusing to reverse to a passing place so that both cars could pass easily.

Mrs Hoddley went on to say that on one occasion when visiting her parents, "I met Mr Smith in the lane; it would have been obvious to any third party, if they had been there, who should back up. Smith just sat there looking at me while talking on his mobile phone. Eventually I reversed back some way until I came to a place where I could pull in. Smith drove towards me and laughed openly. I wound down my window to tell him how childish he was and he simply spat at me and shouted abuse before I could say anything. What makes people like that tick? They've not got one ounce of regard or respect for fellow human beings. The Smith family are a law unto themselves."

The Williams property had sold at auction last week at £100,000 less than its estimated value. A spokesman for the property auctioneers commented, "It was a very desirable property, but sadly its recent history may have been reflected in the price." It has been rumoured that Stephan Smith has bought the Williams' bungalow.

I turned to the picture of Smith's mansion again, and studied it more closely. The place came across as a tackier, scruffier version of Gracelands. You could see how Smith's estate engulfed the Williams' modest home, and I could only imagine the couple's anguish in finding themselves living next door to that shower of shit. The article finished by listing some of the 300 crimes that, between them, the seven members of the Smith household had committed over three decades. The newspaper had attempted to ask Stephan Smith for a comment on recent events, but had received instead a torrent of abuse from a woman believed to be Tanya Smith, Smith's mother.

I closed the page, folded the paper and placed it on the table.

"There's a write-up in this paper too, Paul." Reg handed me the paper, in which a page and a half had been devoted to the cruel twist of fate suffered by the Williams. The story told the same sorry tale as the previous paper. There were three pictures: one of Doris and Jack Williams, one of Stephan Smith receiving his lottery cheque, and a third of the entrance to Smith's mansion. Sick and tacky was the only way to describe what I was looking at. Two statues of pitbull terriers bearing their teeth and sporting black spiky collars took pride of place at the top of the white painted brickwork columns. Artwork on the metal gates also portrayed a pair of fighting dogs, with the words underneath inviting visitors to enter at their own risk. A home-made sign warning 'Beware of the dog' had been crudely painted in red and hung from the gate. If a competition for bad taste ever needed an outright winner, Stephen Smith would be crowned as champion.

Both papers covered the story well, but the second article had dug a little deeper by listing some of the crimes that the family had committed. Manslaughter, GBH, drug deals and twenty-two separate counts of their dogs fouling public places, to name a few, but less than three years spent in prison between them. That such a catalogue of crime had been inflicted on law-abiding citizens without due punishment was an insult.

I stared at the picture of Smith clutching his £56 million cheque, before folding the paper and placing it on top of the other.

"You alright, old boy?" asked Reg.

I nodded that I was fine, but inside I was simply confused, still trying to come to terms with that animal not only having won £56 million but also being allowed to keep it. Ludicrous!

"Quite an impressive CV, if you are looking for someone to defecate on your head from a great height." Reg's comment summed up the Smiths' catalogue of crime in a jovial way. I smiled in agreement. I noticed that rape was not listed and felt that an explanation was in order. I had never spoken of that day, of losing my business, or the death of both Alison's mother and my own. The weeks and months that had followed, watching my wife and daughter trying to come to terms with their ordeals, these were memories I had bottled up inside me until now. Whatever the reason it suddenly felt right to tell an almost complete stranger the chapter of events that had taken place three years previously – events that had almost destroyed me and my family.

"I feel I owe you an explanation as to why there is no mention of the rape in any newspaper," I said.

"Not necessary, Paul."

Reg was being polite. He realised that I finally wanted someone to pour out my heart to. It's sad how easy it is to talk about a problem or how you're feeling to a doctor, psychiatrist or a complete stranger, rather than explain it to someone you love – but that's because you love them.

Clasping my coffee cup with both hands, I tried to keep my shaking out of view. After a couple of sips, my whole body felt strange. Something between nervousness and uncertainty seemed to be running through my veins. I knew why it was. Like the well-worn saying, 'You can run but you can't hide'.

Without asking whether I drank alcohol, Reg ordered two glasses of brandy, speaking in fluent Catalan, the local language. Charlotte and Alison were fluent, but I only knew enough just to get by. Yet again, Reg had done the right thing.

The taste of the brandy brought me back, back to the Catalan church square on a bright November morning.

On the terrace, a young couple had been taking breakfast at a nearby table. As they got up to leave, a scruffy white pigeon landed on their table, looked across at both of us, before digging in to flaky croissants.

"Cheeky little bugger," Reg proclaimed. His timing couldn't have been better.

"It's because of one of those little fellows that my family ended up here," I said. "We even named our smallholding after him or her, *Pichón*."

Reg's face was a picture of confusion.

"Please let me explain," I suggested.

"Annus horribilis is how our Queen described her worst year. To be honest I could have chosen stronger words. Our annus horribilis started at 7.30am on the seventeenth of January 2003, a wet Monday morning, with a phone call from Stan Proline, one of my site managers, who was running the Kingsley Shopping Mall development. He rang to tell me that a sign had been hung on the main entrance saying 'Site closed until further notice' and that all contracts were to contact this number. I knew straightaway what it meant. I.K. Limworth Construction had gone under, taking a million pounds of my money in man hours and materials. You see, Reg, before I was a smallholder I ran a plumbing and heating company started by my father. We employed more than a hundred staff. It was a blow. Downsizing would be the only way to stay afloat, keeping thirty staff on, twenty on site and the rest in the office. We soldiered on until May twenty-sixth when my accountant and friend rang me for an investors' meeting. It turned out that a company that we'd had contracts with for over thirty years was struggling to pay its bills again. I didn't see it coming, and lost a further four hundred and fifty thousand.

"At the same time my mother, who had suffered with cancer for more than twenty years, passed away. My interest and love of a family business and anything to do with plumbing and heating became insignificant. So I made a decision to sell up. Fortunately, we owned the land and the property, office and warehouse, which we sold for development. All the debts were paid including redundancies – some of the staff had been with the company for over forty years. I think that was the hardest part of closing the company down, losing my friends and work colleagues.

"September was when we – well, Alison to be exact – received our next blow. She was deputy head of our local secondary school, where she had worked since qualifying as a teacher in her early twenties. The only time spent away from the school was when she took out a few years when Otis and Charlotte were born. Financially she didn't need to work, she just loved her job. On September the sixth, the first day of the new term, Alison was on dinner duty when a fight broke out between two teenage girls. Alison intervened to break it up, received a bloody nose and was knocked to the ground in the process. The smaller of the two girls also ended up on the ground whereupon she received a continuous kicking. My wife had no choice but to use force, pulling the aggressor away by her hair. In doing so, not intentionally, she pulled a mass of hair and along with it skin leaving a very bloody bald patch. Subsequently, an independent inquiry was started and Alison was suspended without pay.

"A week later, Alison's mother died unexpectedly, after falling down a flight of stairs. Like me, Alison was an only child and had been very close to her mother. I remember thinking to myself, what else can this year bring? Otis, that's our son, was staying with us. He had just finished a two-year tour of duty in Ethiopia and had decided after nine years in the army to continue his career on Civvy Street."

Reg sipped on his brandy and didn't comment. I took a larger swig from my glass as I would need to get through the next part of our annus horribilis. I had never spoken of that afternoon. They say time is a great healer. I suppose that's partly true, but seeing Smith's face today it felt as close as yesterday. For a few minutes my emotions ran high, driven by the guilt that haunted me... for never taking revenge for the wrongs of that creature and his foul family.

"It was three years last week – the sixteenth of November, 2003 – that Stephan Smith with his elder brother Simon, and cousin Allan Smith, broke into our house. Alison and I arrived home at about 3.30pm after our weekly shopping trip. Our front door was wide open and there were CDs and DVDs scattered all over our drive. An empty, sick, drained feeling is how it feels before anger kicks in, when you first realise you've been burgled. Alison was beside herself. Our front room was like a bombsite – the TV, stereo, computer. Anything small and valuable was taken, everything else was trashed. Every cupboard was open and its contents just thrown across the floor. Even the caskets bearing our mothers' ashes had been opened and the contents scattered around the room. I told Alison to ring the police, then Otis arrived while I went to check upstairs... ." I broke off in appreciation of the Spanish custom for drinking brandy. Reg had ordered me a refill, so I took refuge in another large sip.

"You alright, old boy?" he inquired.

I could feel a misty film slipping over my eyes; it was 'the time before tears', as it's often referred to. A spotless and neatly folded light blue handkerchief was placed in front of me. I took it and dabbed my eyes. "Sorry," I said.

"No need for apologies." Reg was without doubt a gentleman.

"You see, Reg, we didn't expect Charlotte to be home. She was meant to be at a sleepover all weekend with a friend from school. Our bedroom and Otis' room had both been vandalised, so I went to check Charlotte's… ." I stopped, finding that I couldn't speak for a second. I bit hard into my bottom lip to stop myself losing it, took another large sip of brandy and resolved to continue.

"The initial shock of actually finding someone in the room startled me until I realised that the blood-stained and naked quivering body that was curled up in the corner belonged to my daughter. I screamed to Alison to call an ambulance, but a mother's intuition had brought her straight up the stairs. I hastily wrapped a sheet around Charlotte, but on seeing her daughter, Alison fell into an uncontrollable panic attack. The seconds between seeing Charlotte and hearing my son's voice were living hell, trying to find ways to comfort the two most important women in my life. As soon as Otis reached the bedroom he took control, tending to his mother and sister, calling the ambulance and maintaining his professional cool. For as long as I live I truly believe that my son's expert handling is what got us through the ordeal.

Charlotte spent two and half weeks in hospital, the first four days in intensive care. Alison spent four weeks in hospital; she had suffered a nervous breakdown. Give me the choice between mental or physical scars, the latter would win every time. When Charlotte and Alison finally returned home, they were completely different to the people I used to know. My son's decision to leave the army had been made for him: for the next three months he became carer to his mother and sister. His medical training was invaluable. Charlotte's ordeal had brought on bed-wetting and nightmares, making nighttimes the worst part to get through. During the day, she and her mother spent most of the day staring at the television. Both refused to go upstairs, so we set up a makeshift bedroom in the dining room. It was like living with two dead people – those vacant, lifeless stares are what upset me the most."

I felt myself losing it again, so I paused for a minute.

"Another coffee, with a brandy?" suggested Reg.

I nodded in agreement.

"I suppose I was being a little bit unfair. Some days would be better than others. Alison might venture in to the kitchen and make a cup of tea or take a vague interest in what the weather was like. Otis and I called them our little glimmers of hope.

"While Alison and Charlotte were still in hospital, two detectives paid me a visit. The police had retrieved a stolen item – a charm bracelet belonging to Alison's mum – which was being hawked around London's East End for scrap value. The amount of charms on the bracelet, some of which included special carats, made one of the jewellers suspicious enough to raise his concerns with the police. The seller, Allan Smith, was identified from the jeweller's CCTV camera. A well-known drug dealer, Smith was known to the police and, along with his brother and cousin, was arrested. After DNA samples were taken, a match was found to the sample taken from Charlotte and identified Stephan Smith as the attacker. What I did on learning this news was something that I've had to live with, but which I still stand by. Hand on heart, I believe I did right by my wife and daughter by declining to press charges." I paused to let this last sentence sink in.

"Surprised?" I asked Reg.

He didn't comment for a few seconds, but then came his reply. "What you did was right and the best thing at that time."

Relieved, I thanked him for his kind words.

"Stephan Smith's defence was that two cars arrived at my home that Saturday afternoon, one with him, his brother and cousin, the other with four complete strangers who they met at the services on the M4. One of the strangers, who they knew as Tom, claimed he had once gone out with Charlotte, and knew our home would make for good pickings. Stephan Smith admitted only to 'consensual sex' with my daughter. In his statement he claimed that he and his relatives had left before the others, and felt that Tom, Charlotte's ex, must have beaten her up. Allan Smith admitted stealing the charm bracelet. The police knew better and advised me that Stephan was an opportunist thief who probably cut through a road in Uxbridge, saw Otis pull out of the drive and went in through the open gate.

"Smith was lying through his back teeth. The police were one hundred percent sure of that. Any jury would convict him for rape, grievous bodily harm and robbery. But for that to happen, Charlotte would have to give evidence and be cross-examined.

At that time she couldn't even say her own name without crying and shaking. I knew that with time and love, Otis and I could bring back our wife, mother, sister and daughter. There was no way I could gamble on putting them through the anguish of a trial simply for the police to get a conviction, for a judge to pass a five-year sentence and for the perpetrator of that crime to be let out on some technicality after serving less two years. No way. I prefer to live with my decision."

A new glass of brandy arrived. I picked it up and drank half straight-down. Reg did the same. The pigeon was still scratching around under the table picking up any scraps.

"He's having a good old tapas session, he must be Spanish," noted Reg.

I couldn't quite raise a smile, as he intended, but nodded in agreement.

"What happened to your pigeon?" asked Reg.

"I hope he's in heaven. That's where he belongs, for the favour he did me and my family. If it wasn't for that little bird I don't know where we would be. As much as I loved the house – we'd lived there for nearly thirty years, it had now become a house not a home. Three months on, Alison and Charlotte were still living and sleeping downstairs. Not once did they venture upstairs. Otis and I talked about moving, and the possible positive effect that a new start might have on the girls. We tried to run it past them on a couple of occasions but simply got no response.

"Okay, the medication they were still on must have played a large part in the vacant stares and lack of interest in anything, but when that pigeon entered the scene… . It had just turned six o'clock in the evening and Otis had taken the girls their supper in the living room. We never sat down together anymore. Alison and Charlotte would venture from the sanctuary of the safe place of the 'bedroom' to the living room and have their meals on two small tables watching – or should I staring at – the television.

"One ring on our clanger of a doorbell was usually loud and long enough to be heard clearly anywhere in the house, but by the time I had reached the front door from the kitchen, the eager call had already rung it three times. On opening the door I was confronted by two well-turned-out children wearing the uniform of the local private school. The girl was about nine, and the boy didn't look more than five.

'Mummy said could you come and stop the water?' asked the girl. I had never had the occasion to speak to my neighbours who had moved in to the largest and most expensive house in the road just over a year ago, but I had often noticed the children in that distinctive uniform going to and fro from the house. The girl explained that water was coming through the ceiling in her mother's bedroom. Her young brother added, 'It's made Mummy say lots of words which we are not allowed to say.'

It was probably the funniest thing that I'd heard in a long time! I grabbed a torch, told Otis what I was doing, and followed the kids back to their house, trying to forget what the boy had said so as not to burst out in a fit of laughter. Arriving at the house I was greeted by an attractive stressed-out thirtysomething, who took me to her bedroom for all the wrong reasons. Water was dripping through the ceiling and buckets were placed around the room to catch the water.

"An old plumber once told me that if you ask a woman where the credit card is, she can tell you straightaway; ask her where the stopcock is and you've no chance of getting the right answer. Ninety percent of the time they are under the sink, so after giving instructions to turn on all the taps in the house and flush all the toilets, I got the little lad to lead me to the kitchen. Fortunately the stopcock was under the sink. I turned it off but the dripping refused to stop, so I went up to the loft, where I met the pigeon and the problem. The cover for the cold water storage tank had been left off, the pigeon had somehow managed to get in the loft, and he had decided to end his days on this Earth in the tank. I could see one of the possible causes of the problem. The pigeon had struggled, for whatever reason, and one of his large feathers had come out and got lodged against the ballcock. The pigeon then must have floated to the overflow causing a blockage. Consequently the tank had overflowed.

I got a plastic bag for the pigeon, the offending feather and a couple of smaller ones which must have come out during his desperate struggle to survive. After placing the pigeon in the outside bin – not much of a send-off, I admit – I went back inside to turn the stopcock back on and explain to the lady of the house what had happened. I was just about to leave when her husband arrived home. After hearing what had happened, he insisted I stay for a drink. Having already refused any payment from his wife, out of courtesy I decided to accept his kind offer.

"Ever since the break-in, I had been hitting the sauce; there weren't many nights that a couple of large malts didn't pass my lips. After Nigel, the husband, had made a gin and tonic for Sue, his wife, and a couple of large malts for us, we three sat around the large kitchen table just talking in general. I couldn't help but notice three carefully laid out rows of estate agents' details alongside a pile of other property details and enquired if they were thinking of moving. Nigel told me his two daughters were heavily into ponies and horses and they were trying to find a property with some land within ten miles of their current home so that the children could stay on at the same school. The girls had read the estate agents' details and placed each property in order of preference, hence the three neat rows. He assumed that the pile of other papers were the rejects but hadn't had time to look at them. While he was speaking, Sue shuffled through the pile, which turned out to be details of smallholdings from all over Europe – not something they wanted, but some estate agents had sent them through anyway.

"I wish the prices were like this for properties over here," said Sue as she showed a couple of sheets to her husband. Nigel flicked through them and passed them to me. I glanced through out of politeness and agreed about the prices. Only when I saw the words 'Mother's Garden' on the last but one property did I stop to absorb the pictures and description more fully.

"The description read: 'Catalan farmhouse, in need of some cosmetic work, in 30 acres of land which includes an ancient vineyard and olive grove. A further property on the land is in need of some extensive work',

"I don't know why I kept hold of that pile of property details; out of politeness, I suppose, as I had no intention of buying abroad. Nigel insisted that I took a few bottles of malt for my trouble that evening, which I did. It wasn't until the next day that I realised what the fruits of my labour the previous evening had yielded. I had arrived back from the shops to find my family discussing which of the 20 or so properties they preferred. To hear Alison and Charlotte string more than three words together about something positive told me instantly that this was the breakthrough Otis and I had been praying for.

Without any intervention from me, all three of them had agreed that 'Mother's Garden' was the favourite and that we should fly out to view the property. Two days later, we were standing outside the house that has now become our home. It was an easy decision to make once I heard my daughter tell her mother and brother which of the four bedrooms was going to be hers. From that moment, I knew that I had got my family back.

"Within a month we had sold our home fully furnished to a letting agents company, and armed with a new Land Rover and trailer, we loaded up our personal possessions and headed off to Mother's Garden, Catalonia, Spain. For nearly three years now my family and I have enjoyed a quality of life which I wish I had sought out earlier. I never thought I would get so excited, so enthusiastic about becoming a smallholder; every hour of every day is pleasurable – from planting rows of lettuces to harvesting clementines and collecting our own free-range eggs. I don't know if our lives are mapped out for us, Reg, but I know one thing. If an opportunity presents itself you have to seize it with both hands."

"I'd have to agree with you there, Paul," replied Reg. "Tell me, does your son still live with you?"

"Yes and no. For the first six months Otis helped me get things straight. Then to help him learn Spanish he took a job at a local pharmacy for a year. Since then he has been at Hospital Universitari de Bellvitge in Barcelona coming down here when he can get away."

"You must be very proud of him."

"Yes, very proud. No father could have asked for a better son, but I have never told him that. I take it for granted that he knows."

"Something I'm a bit confused about though... ."

"What's that, Reg?"

"About the names 'Pichón' and 'Mother's Garden' – which one did you call your home in the end?"

I laughed. It was the one thing the four of us had never agreed on, so we decided to use both names. "There's a second building on our land," I explained, "a tumbledown house with cobbled outbuildings at the far end of the olive grove. I like to think one day that either Otis or Charlotte will meet someone and use it as their family home. The truth of the matter is, I think that will be a long time coming."

"Why do you think that?" Reg asked.

"Well, Otis is dedicated to his profession, always has been, first and foremost. That's not to say he hasn't got an eye for a pretty girl, as my Gran would say. As for Charlotte, after what happened she has never shown any interest in the opposite sex. I think a relationship scares her, which is understandable after what she went through. I've never said this to anyone Reg, but if she told me she was gay it wouldn't worry me. It's going to take a special person for her to regain her confidence completely. Don't get me wrong, she has made some great friendships since coming to Spain, from her college and her work. She plays both the cello and violin. I'm always joking with her and her mates – I call them the 'Queeny Girls'. It's the one thing, if I'm honest, that Alison still worries about."

"I'm a great believer there is someone for everyone," said Reg, "I'm sure she will meet her Prince Charming one day."

"I do hope so."

"If you don't mind me asking, what's the chicken wire for?" I asked, bringing the conversation back to the real world.

"We've decided to increase our chicken stock from six to thirty; somehow I need to divide our garden from the orchard so they can roam to their hearts' content."

"Well, I might be able to help you there. In my barn there are twenty rolls of chicken wire still in their polythene. They've been there a few years, but they are dry so they will still be okay to use. You are more than welcome to them."

"Well, let me give you something for them," I offered gratefully.

"Well, there is a favour you might be able to help me with. I hope you don't think I'm cheeky, but would your trailer accommodate a three-seater settee?"

"No problem."

"It's just that I am having some furniture brought over from the UK at three on Thursday, and it's being delivered to my good friend Malle, who owns the local restaurant bar down on the main road. There is no way that a lorry could drive the eight kilometres to my farm, as it is deep in the mountains. I could ask one of my two neighbours, and they wouldn't hesitate to help me, but with the greatest respect to both of them, past experience of furniture handling nearly always involves a small crisis. Don't get me wrong, Paul, the two families are respectful and I have grown to love them, but a tractor, a trailer and my furniture simply don't mix well!"

I was pleased to help my newfound Good Samaritan. Not only had he averted a major crisis today, he had listened to me with compassion and understanding. I didn't feel better about talking about our annus horribilis, but I started to feel different – only to be expected when remembering sad or bad times.

As Reg drew a map of how to find his local restaurant, I asked how he had come to live in Catalonia. I was quite taken aback by his reply.

"The same reason as you, Paul. A lame bird, a lame bird of the metal variety. I used to be Captain Reginald Howard Challenger and fly long-haul. On account of several personal issues, I asked to be transferred to short haul to allow me more time at home. During this time I needed to make every pilot's worst nightmare, an emergency landing, at Pens."

Pens was the first major town after the border on the south coast. I knew it well, as Alison's best friend Jill had twice flown in there when she was unable to fly into Girona, the main airport.

"The passengers were taken on to their destination and we were grounded for five days while repairs and checks were carried out on the aircraft. My co-pilot and crew took off for the French Riviera for a few days but I decided to hire a car and head over the border to nowhere in particular and ended up in Angies. I can remember it like it was yesterday, Paul. I decided to walk off my evening meal before returning to my hotel, browsing in the shop windows as I went. The one and only estate agent in Angies was squashed in between a shoe shop and a gun shop – in fact, that gunsmith is now a good friend of mine. I had no intention of buying a property in England, Spain or anywhere else in the world. I could only string together a few words of Spanish at the time. I brushed away the film of dust on the windows to study the properties being advertised. A notice displaying the agent's opening hours – Thursday, Friday and Saturday between six and eight o'clock – indicated that the property market in this area was as buoyant as the rest of the world in the late eighties. It was the last property, a farm, that took my eye, for no other reason at first but for its commercial value. The price was 30,000 pesetas. It had plenty of investment potential, mainly woodland, was approximately 100 acres in size and yielded an annual income of 2,000 pesetas. I didn't have a pen or paper with me and, in those days, carrying a mobile phone was armbreaking so I had left it at the hotel.

The following day, I returned to the estate agents out of curiosity, to get the phone number. Although it was only ten in the morning, there was someone inside, so I went in to find out more. Fortunately, the estate agent spoke better English than I did Spanish at that time and he carefully explained why the property was so cheap. The fact was that apart from one barn the house and other buildings were complete wrecks. The last people had left more than ten years ago; there was no electricity, no running water and the nearest neighbour was six kilometres away. Undeterred, I decided to view the property. To cut a long story short, I bought the place. I hope on Thursday you will see it and agree why I had to buy it."

I must confess I was mildly unenthralled at the prospect. Glancing ahead, I saw Alison and Charlotte appear with bags hanging from every arm. Reg laughed at what two women in a clothes shop might yield. As they had been gone closer to an hour, it was decided that the girls would skip their special Hossa coffee this week, so as not to miss out on our weekly treat of menu of the day back in our home village. With Alison and Charlotte present, I was unable to express my thanks and appreciation to Reg for listening to me and my problems, but it's surprising how much a handshake and eye contact can convey. After confirming our three o'clock appointment for Thursday, Reg headed off in the opposite direction for a meeting with an antique dealer about some books.

During our drive to the restaurant, Alison asked me about my conversation with Reg. Taking care what I relayed, I told her that we had talked about the usual things – football, cricket and politics mainly. I was taken aback when Alison said "I suppose you scanned through his paper?"

Before she had time to finish, I hastily recounted how, according to the sports page, my old club, Spurs, were doing well. Since moving here, Otis and I had adopted Barcelona as our home team.

In the thirty-two years that Alison and I had been married I had never lied or even had the slightest intention of doing so, but in the space of a few minutes I had just done so twice. The Spanish call it a 'penochi'. I took a quick glance in the mirror to check myself, little knowing how many times I would repeat that act in the coming months.

CHAPTER TWO

I CAN CLEARLY REMEMBER THE FIRST TIME I MET FRANCIS. Two waitresses and the restaurant owner's wife watched spellbound as he climbed down from his lorry cab and made his way across the road to enter the restaurant. Hollywood's finest would be lucky to hold an audience like that.

He certainly wasn't what I expected a lorry driver to look like, that's for sure. I'm not saying that lorry drivers are an ugly breed of men, but Francis definitely didn't fit that category. He just didn't act or carry himself like a man who had just spent seven days and nights driving and sleeping in the cab of a forty-foot articulated lorry.

The restaurant and bar were open plan, and as we were the only two customers he made his way over to our table. Reg got up from his seat and greeted Francis with a firm handshake.

"Find us okay?" he asked.

"Yes thanks. Sorry I'm running a bit late. Strong winds in the last hour slowed me down to almost a snail's pace. I reckon we're in for a storm."

Reg nodded in agreement and then turned to introduce me to Francis.

"This is my friend Paul. He has been kind enough to loan me his trailer to complete the last part of the journey," Reg explained.

Francis extended his hand and we exchanged handshakes.

"I'm just going to grab a quick coffee before we set off again if that's okay?"

Francis had been briefed back in England that he would probably be involved in helping on the last leg of the journey. He invited both Reg and me to join him and ordered three large coffees in word-perfect Spanish from the restaurant owner's wife, who was still gazing in admiration at him. Francis took the prolonged stares in his stride and seemed unaware of the effect he was having on the local women. Even so, you could understand why within such a short space of time he had all the ladies laughing – he was one of those men who seemed to ooze charisma from every pore.

I was finding it hard to get my head around the way he was dressed. I suppose white T-shirt, jeans, bomber jacket and desert boots were what I was expecting… but Francis was nothing like that. Immaculately turned out, his clothes looked like they were straight off the peg. There was something else about him too, yet I couldn't quite put my finger on it. The way he preened his hair – Francis had a fine head of shoulder-length, auburn hair that would have made quite a few women envious. Looking back I should have pushed myself beyond my preconceptions. I later learnt that he was 31, although I would have said no more than early twenties. After we had paid for the coffees and made our way towards the exit, all three ladies kissed goodbye to Francis on the cheek as a sign of their affection… I thought it looked more like a case of lust.

I didn't realise a three-seater settee could be so heavy. While Reg and I struggled at one end, Francis managed with some ease on his own at the other end. All three settees were handmade to order and although they were well covered in plastic, you could easily see the quality of manufacture. Once we had managed to load them on the trailer and tied them down securely we set off for Reg's farm up in the hills.

We had done less than half a mile when Reg gave me directions to do a right turn. I was pleasantly surprised when I saw the unmade road, as it was not nearly as bad as the farmtrack which he had described. It was quite wide enough for two vehicles to pass each other, and the surrounding countryside at this point was made up mostly of fields of crops, interspersed with woodland.

The scenery changed dramatically once we reached the first of the farm buildings that belonged to Reg's neighbours, the Romma family. The road narrowed considerably and the fields turned into dense forest. My speed was down to 10 miles an hour. We had gone about two miles along the track when Reg pointed out his second neighbour, Hossa, the eldest son of Manuel Romma. As we passed, we were greeted by a selection of farmyard animals including ducks, chickens, bantams and four of the scruffiest mongrel dogs you have ever seen. The collective barks, clucks and quacks made quite a racket.

"That's my nearest neighbour when I need to borrow a cup of sugar!"

Reg turned to me and smiled. I would shortly learn the reason for that comment along with the smile.

"I've had a few good sessions with the Rommas over the years. A quick drink and a chat to them always run into a meal and some serious drinking. They are lovely people."

The road was very uneven and narrow from then on. The

majority of the journey was a steady climb, but every so often the dirt track would make a sudden descent into a valley, where we would have to negotiate a ford. Some were dry, while others carried a healthy flow of water. I could quite understand how Reg's farm got its name, *La Granja Oculta* or The Hidden Farm. We were just coming up to our fifth mile on the safari when something stood in our path. It was a delicacy that many Catalan restaurants serve and which I had sampled on a couple of occasions. From the noise they were making I realised we were facing not one but eight wild boar, who were distinctly not dead nor lying on a plate in the way that I usually met them. I looked over to Reg for guidance.

"Don't worry! Just toot your horn and drive on."

"Easier said than done," I muttered to myself, as I made my way forward. Two of the larger boars made it quite clear that they didn't like my attitude. They were pushing their snouts up against the side windows, exposing their vicious-looking teeth. I could almost feel their breath on me as we came face to face, their teeth grating against the window. Two thoughts ran through my mind: one, I hoped they couldn't tell that I had dined on their ancestors in the past, and two, I hoped to God we didn't break down.

"When you run out of sugar do you walk to your neighbours, Reg?" I asked.

"I only walk this road if I am with my two dogs and a gun," he replied. "I always keep a shotgun, well hidden, in the Land Rover just in case. Occasionally I've been caught out, but a quick phone call and one of the Rommas always comes to my rescue. You see all the forest we are passing through? It belongs to the

Rommas and me. The wood alone brings in some money and then we make a further income from the wild boar by selling their meat to the restaurants in the area. The Rommas run the whole thing and I just take a percentage each year. We've worked together like this for the last twenty years and it suits us all fine."

Reg certainly had his head screwed on regarding the financial side of things. What I couldn't get my head around was why someone would want to live in a place that only a recluse would consider. Reg didn't strike me as some kind of hermit. Well, one thing was for sure – he definitely had the longest, bumpiest drive that I'd ever ridden on. Ever since leaving the main road, I'd been getting more and more curious about what Reg's farm would be like. As it came into view, I could tell that I was not going to be disappointed.

Time appeared to have stood still for over a century as we entered the courtyard. It took my breath away, as I quickly realised there were two stories here. The farmhouse had been lovingly restored; it was quite a large house and oozed character and charm. A stone wall circled the whole front of the house, protecting the perfectly manicured lawns and borders. I half expected a wild boar to come charging towards us at any minute. A wooden arch that supported two gates marked one end of a crazy-paved path that led up to the entrance of the house. It was as if a little corner of England had relocated to Spain.

In sharp contrast to the rest of the farm were two large barns to the right of the house, one of which was virtually a pile of rubble. The whole roof had caved in and the front and most of the sidewalls had collapsed. The other barn still had walls and a roof but was crying out for some TLC. Weeds and grasses up to four-feet high and young pine trees seemed to spring up everywhere. Only Reg's constant driving in and reversing across the patch had stopped this onslaught of vegetation taking over. It was almost as if the forest had sneaked in uninvited and was trying to take hold.

"How on earth did they get here?." Francis was looking at what I thought was a row of sheds cowering beneath the sprawling climbers. On closer inspection I could see that the sheds were in fact six shipping containers. The two of us sat and waited for Reg's explanation. Given that the road we had driven down was only just passable by a four-wheel drive, how on Earth could a container lorry have attempted the journey? Reg laughed at our puzzled expressions.

"The reason for those containers being here is down to the determination and lunacy of a young entrepreneur and my good fortune in meeting him," he said, and was promptly interrupted by the sound and subsequent arrival of two golden Labradors. The smaller of the two dogs came round to my side of the vehicle and barked loudly at me.

"They don't get to see many people," Reg explained. He got out of the vehicle and called out to the dog, "Spear, that's enough." The guard dog stopped barking and took off to join his mate. The restaurant owner had handed Reg a plastic bag just as we were leaving. It contained some lamb bones which the owner always saved for his customer's dogs. As soon as each dog had a bone securely clamped in its mouth, the pair sloped off into the long grass. Francis had already got out of the car and was heading towards the containers for a closer look.

"Don't worry, Paul," said Reg, "They won't bite. In truth they are more likely to lick you to death, but they are great company and keep the wild boar away."

I could see that the two dogs served Reg well, both as guard dogs and as companions.

"I like the name Spear, what's the other one called?" I asked.

A cheeky grin appeared on Reg's face and I knew that a joke, witty remark or anecdote was about to be served on me.

"Shake," he replied.

"I see you're fascinated with those containers and how they came to be here," Reg called over to Francis.

"I'm a bit puzzled, yes," said Francis, keen to hear the rest of the tale.

Reg obliged. "Originally, my belongings were meant to arrive in three forty-foot containers, but because of weight restrictions we ended up using six instead. They were to be left in one of the Rommas' fields as you come off the main road, with one container arriving from Barcelona port each day. I realised that no lorry driver would risk their vehicle in an attempt to reach my house with the containers, so I planned to gradually transport my stuff via the Land Rover once the renovations on the house were completed. I'd already agreed to buy the containers outright because the shipping company said it wasn't worth their while shipping them back to England empty."

"On the day of the final delivery, I went down to meet the driver. It wasn't the usual chap, but a crazy young chancer is how I would best describe him. We got chatting and I explained how I intended to transfer my goods up to the farm. Once we'd finished unloading, I invited him up to the house for a drink. On the way, I'd noticed that he was closely studying the track, then to my surprise when we reached the farm he simply said 'Give me 400 euro and I'll get all six containers up to the farm for you'! It was a done deal, there and then. We agreed he would come back the next day and perform the impossible."

"True to his word, the driver appeared the following morning accompanied by three lorries and drivers, a cargo trailer and a breakdown truck fitted with a large winch. It was the most bashed-up old vehicle I'd ever seen. It had no windows or doors and certainly didn't look capable of driving in a straight line let alone up a mountain. It turned out that my crazy chancer had started his own haulage business about four years ago and now had quite a fleet of vehicles. The smashed-up unit had been his first vehicle which he now used for moving trailers around the yard. It was called Trabaje Caballo, or workhorse, and certainly lived up to its name over the next eight hours – which is how long it took to get all six containers up to the farm."

"Fair play to your chancer," said Francis, "he deserves every success with that kind of determination."

"Too true," I agreed.

"Right, gentlemen," said Reg, "now let me show you my home."

There was definitely an air of England's green and pleasant pastures about the place. A white picket gate opened on to a carpet of green lawn bordered by flowering shrubs. Hanging baskets adorned the walls at regular intervals and a rustic birdbath took centre stage. An apexed tiled-roof porch housed two worn oak bench seats and led invitingly to the front door. The whole scene would not have looked out of place on the front of a chocolate box.

Reg opened the front door without using a key.

"Don't you bother with locking up then, Reg?" I asked.

"No point Paul. If someone is going to take the trouble of getting past forest, wild boar, dirt tracks and my two labs barking or licking them to death, then a locked door won't deter them."

Point taken.

Two full suits of armour stood guard as we walked into the hallway. On the floor there was a well-worn, but obviously expensive, rug of orange and red hues, which brought a warm brightness. A grandfather clock and table bearing a Tiffany lamp stood under the stairs, which ran for about twenty steps before reaching the landing where we could see another coat of armour.

Reg led us through to a large open-plan lounge, diner and kitchen, where we made ourselves comfortable in a couple of large overstuffed leather settees which faced a wide stone fireplace, well-stocked with piles of logs to either side. It was all so wonderfully traditional. A slick-looking laptop sat atop an Edwardian desk, the only reminder in the room that we were definitely in the 21st century.

Reg took a few moments to rekindle the fire, while telling us how he kept it alight from the first of October and let it go out on the first of April, in the tradition of the monks in the monastery at St Trallis, a small town in the heart of the Pyrenees. Once the fire had developed a warm glow, he invited us through the kitchen to the conservatory and opened a set of double doors to the outside. There was no need for further explanation, as the eighth wonder of the world stretched out in front of us. From here it was plain to see why Reg had fallen in love with the place – the view. Topped by whitish pink snow-drenched peaks, the blue-grey rocks and cliffs of the Pyrenees descended into a valley of trees which dived and curved over hills and dips right up to where we were standing. The view of the mountains and surroundings in all their glory was breathtakingly spectacular.

"With a blue sky or sunset it makes you want to take up painting to try to capture the beauty," said Reg.

I knew where he was coming from. It was a grey overcast day, yet the view was still magnificent. I made a mental note to get Alison invited over to witness the sight one day; I knew she would fall in love with it.

Suddenly a flash of lightning lit up the dark afternoon sky. I was fixed to the spot and wanted to watch the spectacular light show unfold, but Reg had something to tell us.

"We've been caught out by the storm, gents, which leaves us two options. If you don't leave before the rain starts you won't get back down to the main road. Those fords we passed become fast-flowing rivers in a very short space of time. Option one is to leave the trailer here and set off now. I could get the Rommas to give me a hand tomorrow and then bring the trailer back to you, Paul, by midday. Option two is that you are both more than welcome to stay the night. I have some excellent Rioja in my cellar, and if I do say so myself, I'm a dab hand in the kitchen. If that's not tempting enough there's a twenty-five year old bottle of malt that doesn't need to get any older. I leave it up to you to decide."

Francis was more than happy to accept Reg's hospitality, having spent the last seven nights sleeping in his lorry. My dilemma was Alison and Charlotte; they hadn't spent a night in the house without me in the last three years. Our dog, Florrie, an old mongrel who came with the house, would be with them and I knew he would lay down his life before letting harm come to any of us. But I still wasn't happy about not being at home, especially with a storm on the way, so I decided to ring Alison and see how she felt. To my surprise, Otis answered the phone. He had been due home that weekend but rarely got time off during the week. It seemed that one of the theatres had had to close on account of technical problems, so he'd been given a couple of days' leave. Once I'd explained my predicament to him, there was nothing else to decide. He reassured me that he had no intention of going anywhere and handed me over to Alison for a quick word. She joked that of course she was going to miss my snoring, farting, waking her to see if she was asleep, pinching the duvet, talking in my sleep... the list went on for several moments, before we said our goodbyes and rang off.

"Looks like you have yourself a couple of house guests, Reg," I announced.

"Great!"

"If we organise ourselves I reckon we could beat that storm and have your three new sofas in here," suggested Francis, looking at us for approval.

"I'm game."

"Well let's go for it then, gents," said Reg.

Within ten minutes we had moved the old settees on to the trailer to take to the second-hand shop. They still looked in reasonable condition and might do someone a favour if they were just starting out.

Each time a settee needed to be moved, Francis took one end

by himself. He had the strength of two men but no muscle to speak of. What's more, there wasn't a single hair on his arms or hands like you'd expect to see on someone with strength.

While Francis and I removed the protective plastic, Reg prepared three glasses of beer, for which I quickly made a beeline. Francis, however, headed for the pile of throws and new cushions that Reg had conjured up and promptly set about doing what most men find impossible, homemaking! A feminine touch is sometimes needed in the simple task of placing a throw or cushions so it looks just right. Our lorry driver was clearly in touch with his feminine flair and soon had the furniture looking cosy and welcoming.

"The only problem we've got tonight is that one of you is going to have to bunk down on one of the new settees, because, believe it or not, I've only got two bedrooms."

I was a bit taken aback. Given the size of the house, I'd expected it to have at least six or so bedrooms. I volunteered to bunk downstairs, as a bed for Francis would have been a very welcome sight.

Reg invited us to explore the upstairs. Reaching the landing, two more suits of armour came into view, guarding a robust doorway like those down in the hall. The first room he showed us was his own, large, and in the Tudor style, complete with a four-poster bed and en-suite. As with the rest of the house, you could tell Reg wasn't the kind of person to compromise when it came to quality and taste.

The next two rooms were filled from floor to ceiling with books. He was clearly one of those people who could never bring themselves to part with a book even once they had read it.

As we made our way back downstairs, my curiosity was running into overdrive trying to guess what was in the guarded rooms. As if he guessed my thoughts, Reg opened the large oak door and flicked on a light switch revealing the cavernous interior and its contents. My curiosity was instantly stunned, shocked and satisfied.

As I learned later, Reg owned one of the finest and largest private libraries in the world. No wonder he hadn't bothered to show us through the door upstairs: a gallery rail that ran the length of the vast room shelved thousands of books which were accessible from both the first and ground floor.

"Like a book or two then, Reg?" quipped Francis.

"Yes, it's a little hobby of mine. Now I'm going to prepare some food and sort out a few bottles of wine, so feel free to have a browse. If you find something of interest, you are more than welcome to borrow them."

It was half an hour before we heard from Reg again to announce "Gentlemen, your supper awaits," before he realised that he couldn't see either of us. Francis had stayed on the ground floor, losing himself in the section at the far end of the library, while I had ventured to the second floor and was wading through the section marked 'Agriculture'. Reg's library was the ultimate Aladdin's cave for anyone who loved reading. Yes, the internet's a great source of information, and no doubt 'experts' predict that books are on their way out, but for me I wouldn't want to live in a world without books. I picked out a book on cottage gardening for Alison and one for myself that promised to tell me everything I'd need to know about poultry.

"I'd love to borrow these two books," said Francis, as he held up copies of *The English Patient* and *She Walked Alone* for Reg to see, "but I don't know when I'll be back down this way. Would you trust me to post them back?"

"Of course," he replied, "I can give you an address back in England to mail them to."

I'd not read either of the books that Francis had chosen, but they looked distinctly too 'romantic' for my taste!

CHAPTER THREE

IN LITTLE MORE THAN HALF AN HOUR Reg had conjured up a veritable feast. I suppose the best way to describe it was like his garden, England meets Spain. Jamon de España next to York ham, olives and pickled onions mingled together, manjar blanco and mature English cheddar side by side on the cheeseboard, and Heinz salad cream standing proudly alongside a bowl of alioli, the Catalan mayonnaise. Accompanied by a large Spanish omelette, mixed salad, fresh ripe tomatoes, asparagus and two bottles of excellent Rioja, Reg's humble spread made an impressive and mouthwatering sight.

Once we had sat down, Reg poured the wine and made a toast of thanks to us both. It turned out that Francis was vegetarian, just like Alison and Charlotte. From there the conversation revolved around food, drink and football, not bad subjects, but something still bothered me about Francis – I just couldn't put my finger on what it was. I subtly tried to pry through conversation hoping to reveal the missing factor, but to no avail. It was like an itch I couldn't scratch, so there was nothing else for it but to be more direct in my questioning. I started off quite innocently by asking how he came to be a long-distance lorry driver.

"I suppose I'd have to put that down to my time spent in the British Army. They put me through my HGV, so when I left the police force seven months ago and found myself at a loose end it seemed like the best job to go for. I signed up with a decent agency and so far I've had plenty of work."

As Reg topped us up with more wine, he enquired which regiment Francis had served with.

"The Paras," replied Francis.

I was stunned. Francis looked even less like a Para than he did a lorry driver! However, he seemed to know instinctively that Reg had also at some time served in one of the services, and so asked Reg the same question. Reg revealed that he had spent 15 years in the RAF as a fighter pilot. From there on, the two men started swapping stories about where they had served.

Now that the ball was rolling, I prepared to step up my investigation of Francis, but Reg neatly beat me to it by asking him why he hadn't stayed on with the police. Francis gave a broad smile before going on to state that the three years he had spent in the force were a great experience and he had thoroughly enjoyed them. Unfortunately some of his colleagues and especially his superiors could not accept that in his spare time he enjoyed cross-dressing. Shock didn't come close to describing how I felt. I nearly choked on my wine!

Reg took it all in his stride. "Ah, cross-dressers were the best stewards a captain could ask for; I still get a Christmas card from some of them now," he added.

While Reg was taking Francis's disclosure on board with the greatest of ease, I was taking some large gulps of wine to cover my shock. At least I now knew why I sensed something different about Francis. Good job he'd told us, as it would have taken me a long time to have ever guessed that secret!

The conversation returned to the time Francis spent in the

police and how his private life had not been the only reason for leaving the force. The way in which the judicial system continually let the bad guys get away with crime, together with the wholly inadequate sentences given for serious criminal offences, had heavily influenced his decision. Francis had clearly been a committed policeman but was defeated by the frustration and anger at watching the law courts become a laughing stock among the criminal community.

"So, whereabouts do you live back in England?" asked Reg.

"Well, until I was seven, we lived in Finchley, London, then we moved to Norfolk with my father's job. My parents still live there today, so home for me at present is my parents' home or a forty-foot lorry. My last job with the police kept me on the move quite a bit though. I was part of a drug-busting team that went tits up. We were tracking a family called Smith – headed up by Stephan Smith, that imbecile who won the Euro lottery about two years ago."

It wasn't so much the mention of his name that made my world stand still for a second, it was the coincidence – so bizarre that it beggared belief – that Stephan Smith should re-enter my life not once but twice in less than a week. Usually a sceptic when it comes to all that supernatural stuff, at that moment I could easily have been persuaded to believe in divine intervention.

Unaware of the shockwaves he had created, Francis helped himself to another slice of Reg's excellent Spanish omelette. It was only when he looked up at both Reg and myself that he realised something was amiss.

"What's up?" he asked.

There was a silence, splintered only by the sound of pine logs cracking in the fire. The three of us looked at one another, each waiting for the other to speak when, to my relief, and seeing a nod from me, Reg took the reins.

"Stephan Smith raped Paul's daughter three years ago," he explained.

"Charlotte Taylor?"

It was a shock to hear Charlotte's name said out loud.

"How come you know my daughter's name?" I asked.

My tone of voice and direct stare must have shown that my protective instincts as a father had been triggered by the mention of Stephan Smith's name. Suddenly I felt threatened by a stranger knowing something so private about my daughter.

Clearly Francis was made of strong stuff. Calmly, and cool as a cucumber, he moved his Spanish omelette to one side of the plate to make way for some salad, which he started to take from the charger as he spoke.

"Last year I could have told you not only the colour but the make of Stephan Smith's underpants." He paused to place his cutlery on his plate and took a sip of wine before speaking again. "Thames Valley had their suspicions that a very large quantity of cocaine was being stored at Smith's mansion. As briefing and liaison officer for the operation, my duty was to study Stephan Smith and his family so that I could brief my colleagues on the team about the type of people we would be dealing with. For that reason, I know everything about what happened to your daughter and the horrific ordeal that your family's been through."

I felt humbled and offered Francis an apology for my defensiveness.

48

Francis smiled in appreciation. "Your experience was terrible but thankfully you have managed to rebuild your lives. People that come up against Smith and his family don't always find the strength to survive."

I noticed that Francis suddenly looked different. The blue eyes had lost their sparkle and a mask of anguish and sadness clouded his face.

"To our knowledge, Smith and his family are responsible for at least fourteen deaths."

It was Reg's turn to speak. "What baffles me, Francis, is how come that individual and his family aren't behind bars if they've caused the loss of that many lives?"

"Eight counts of manslaughter – all vehicle-related – but six were not proven. The rest all resulted from bad drugs they had supplied."

"So what I've read in the tabloids is true. You're saying that thanks to our judicial system, Smith and his family have served less than four years for more than a dozen murders and numerous other crimes? I find that absolutely scandalous!" There was no mistaking the controlled rage in Reg's voice.

Francis nodded in agreement. "When my chief inspector gave me the job, he also asked if I would consider doing an analysis report on the Smith family, as I'd got experience of doing these in the army."

"You're an analyst?"

"Yes."

"An analyst in Her Majesty's forces?"

"Yes," he confirmed.

I was taken aback. Was there no end to this man's talents?

A policeman, lorry driver, paratrooper, and now an analyst!

"Being given the job of analysing the Smith family was the toughest task that I've ever been assigned. Precisely three hundred and eighty-two crimes ranging from the relatively petty, such as non-payment of parking fines, to manslaughter. I read more than a hundred and fifty personal letters from victims. Brave innocents expressing their anger at being let down by the courts. And they were right... and yet, even I have to admit that the chances of getting any of the cases against this family to court are unlikely, let alone achieving a conviction. Let me give you an example."

Francis paused for a moment to gather his thoughts, then took a long sip of wine before telling us more.

"At just seventeen, Stephan Smith mounted the pavement in a stolen car and hit a young mother and her child. Simon Granger, the bereaved husband, was so overwhelmed with grief that he took his own life. That is all fact – nothing more, nothing less. Smith served less than twelve months because the police were accused of driving erratically in their pursuit of him. The guidelines for car chases changed dramatically after that case but that's no consolation to the Granger family."

My mind was a mixture of emotions: the pain of my own hell caused by Smith swirled around with the heartache of so many of his other victims. Although his manner and voice remained calm and professional, I sensed that Francis still held a lot of anger towards that family. The person that had stepped out of the lorry cab earlier today was certainly delivering some interesting revelations.

By now Francis had moved on to Stephan's Smith's involvement in drug pushing. He told us that they had dealt in everything: cocaine, speed, ecstasy, crack, heroin – the works. Worse still, whenever a bad batch of drugs hit the streets, more often than not it could be traced back to the Smiths, but the links were never strong enough to be proved.

"They're not dealing any more though?" Reg asked.

"You must be kidding, they're in even deeper nowadays," replied Francis.

I could see from the expression on Reg's face that we shared the same disbelief about this bunch of bastards. There was no point in being polite about these people – they simply didn't deserve it.

"Are you telling me that since they won all that money they still insist on dealing drugs?"

"I'm afraid so," replied Francis.

"But why?" Reg asked.

"Greed? Power? Playing the bully? Staying on top as Mr Big? Take your pick," suggested Francis. You have to remember that this family had a reputation before it won its millions. They loved the life they led. Winning a lot of money doesn't stop you being a dickhead; if anything, in their case it enhanced their lifelong habits. They still steal from supermarkets, refuse to pay maintenance, let their dogs foul in public places and park in disabled bays."

Francis stopped suddenly, shutting his eyes tightly for a few seconds and then opening them again.

"Going back to those letters, I remember one of the saddest ones came from a son whose elderly mother suffered with arthritis and walked with a zimmer frame. While out with Bert, her husband, on their weekly trip to the local supermarket, they were forced to park at the outer limits of the car park because all the disabled bays were full. Nearing the entrance of the supermarket, Bert noticed two men loading packs of beer into the boot of their BMW, which was parked in a disabled bay. It was clear that neither of the men was disabled, so he took it upon himself to point out, politely, that they really shouldn't be parked there. The verbal abuse and threats that were hurled at the elderly couple were frightening and venomous. You'll have guessed by now that the abusers were no less than Smith and one of his cousins. Not content with displaying their filthy language, Smith proceeded to let one of his dogs out of the car and provoked it to snarl and growl at the couple as they edged away from the scene and took refuge in the supermarket. The damage was done though. Later that day, distraught and distressed, the mother suffered a stroke and died the same evening in hospital. While at her bedside, Bert told his son what had happened and broke down in shame that he had not been able to defend her from their attackers. Bert passed away the following day.

We all sat in grim silence for a few moments, reflecting on the miserable tale that Francis had shared with us. As usual, Reg was the first to speak.

"How does this man repeatedly flout the law? It is utter madness. These individuals should be incarcerated. Surely that drugs bust should have sent them down? A crack team of police officers and you didn't get a conviction?"

"It never happened," Francis said. "A serious coach crash on the way to the operation meant the whole thing was called off. My report with analysis on the Smith family was handed over to Thames Valley police. A raid took place three months later, which I wasn't involved in, and I know there have been subsequent attempts since then. I haven't read or heard if any were successful since leaving the force but I'm pretty sure the tabloids would have been on the case if our celebrity piece of shit had finally been flushed out.

"I agree with you, Reg. The likes of Stephan Smith and his family should be locked up and the key thrown away but, of course, our softly-softly approach to criminals in our country would never allow that. In my humble opinion, people like Smith will never treat the law with any respect while there's no decent deterrent in place. You want an example of what I mean, I'll give you one."

Francis was firmly astride his hobby horse now and nothing was going to stop him.

"There used to be a nasty piece of work on my patch called David Rossly. He was no way in Smith's league, but still he was an undesirable. Car theft was his speciality. When he was up in court for being in possession of a stolen vehicle once again, his solicitor confidently predicted that a hundred hours' community service was the maximum he would get. Unfortunately for Rossly, the judge's daughter had had her car stolen the previous day, so sympathy for car thieves was in short supply at the hearing. The judge handed down the maximum he could give, which was a two-year custodial sentence. Rossly's face was a picture. He was physically sick once he got to his cell. The cocky lad who walked into that courtroom was certainly not evident as he sat alone awaiting a two-year stretch. That day, real justice was done!"

"…And of course the other problem is, time after time

known criminals walk free after months of police work because a judge hasn't got the courage to hand down the right sentence or because witnesses don't turn up – they're just too frightened to show their faces in court."

I knew Francis was having a dig at me for not letting Charlotte take the stand, and I could see his point. People like Smith's continually got away with their crimes because the cases never got as far as court, but I wanted to hear more.

"So in your analysis, Francis, how would you sum up my decision to not allow justice to be done?"

"In all honesty, Paul, I believe you took the right course of action at the time."

I felt reassured to hear that answer from someone who was fast earning my respect, and prompted Francis to expand a little more.

"I'm glad you think it was the right course of action, but why?"

Francis smiled, "Because in your case the charge of robbery was pursued and won. Which was fortunate because the rape of your daughter would never have stood up in court."

"What? Are you trying to suggest that it never happened?" I spluttered, my hackles rising sharply again.

"No, nothing like that Paul," replied Francis, as calm as ever. "What I'm saying is that in my professional opinion, putting your daughter on the stand would have been a waste of time and resources."

At this point Reg lent over and topped up our glasses once more, giving me a reassuring nod to check I was alright.

"What right have you or your colleagues to say the rape of my daughter didn't warrant time or resources?" I asked as calmly as I could.

"Please, Paul," said Francis, "what I'm about to tell you, you might not want to hear. Nevertheless, they are the facts."

Reg looked across at me again, as if to say 'Stay calm, you're among friends'.

"Have you two ever heard of podders?"

Reg and I both shook our heads.

"Well you won't find it in any English dictionary, but it's the word we use to describe someone who not only admits to a crime but also does time for it when they have never actually committed or had any involvement with the crime! As you might expect, podders are not the sharpest tools in the box, which makes them the perfect utensil for each and every one of the Smiths' crimes. They steal, they smuggle and they do time for that family without a second thought."

A horrible thought struck me. "So are you saying that when Stephan Smith rapes a girl... ."

"No, Paul." Francis could see where my thoughts were leading. "He reserves that 'entertainment' for himself, but he always wears protection to cover his tracks. It's just his way of saying 'I'm top dog round here and don't you forget it'. Hurting people is like water off a duck's back to him."

I could not quite believe what I was hearing: it was so completely alien to my own world and the values that I held.

Francis continued. "Getting a Smith convicted would be like winning the lottery. How ironic is that! Even before Smith's win, he kept his back fully covered thanks to David Buxton, a solicitor whose morals fall well short of his profession and the faithful service of his podders. Their one fear in that family is being locked away, so they'll do whatever it takes to avoid it. I can't remember who went down for the theft of your belongings, but it was a podder who took most of the blame. It's nothing to them to do six months to a five-year stretch, at the worst. After all, if you get five years you will be out in two years on a tag, plus twenty grand and a clapped-out BMW convertible courtesy of the Smiths. Winning the lottery was a stepping stone – an almighty one – for Smith. He's ambitious and determined, so the lump sum has given him the green light to becoming 'Mr Big'."

"The whole family's attitude to all that is decent is revolting. With that kind of money behind them, they have provided the undeniable evidence that crime does pay."

"So Stephan Smith and his cronies can rape, steal, murder and still walk away? Is the law completely powerless?" I asked in despair.

"I've told you the facts, Paul. To date, that is exactly how it seems," replied Francis grimly.

"And these are the people the Euro lottery rewards with a prize that's worth millions?" queried Reg.

"I think that's a different issue, Reg."

"You disagree with that? You don't think the money should have been confiscated and shared out between his victims, let say?"

"Reg, you and I will have to agree to disagree on this one; I've been down that road too many times," said Francis wearily.

However, Reg was not about to drop the matter.

"So you're saying it's fine for pieces of shit like that to be given millions to finance their illegal ways?"

We were all at it now – even Reg. The discussion had heated our tempers and exhausted our patience such that it was impossible for us to use anything but expletives when it came to talking about the Smith family.

"Look Reg, he bought the ticket, he won. Nothing can be done on that score. Besides which, trying to compensate his victims would prove difficult given that so many of the cases never actually made it to court or were proved."

"Well I for one would have no problem blowing that scum's head off his shoulders if I thought I could retrieve the money for his victims."

"Then that would be murder and theft," Francis thoughtfully pointed out.

"Well I could live with that in this instance," said Reg fiercely.

Reg clearly had a bee in his bonnet about the Smiths.

"I'm not defending Smith and his clan; if I thought for one minute taking out Smith or members of that family was the right thing to do I would have sanctioned it. It would be good for the country and mankind, but we must never stoop to their level."

"You're right."

These two men had locked horns but out of respect and because they were gentlemen they unlocked and stepped back a pace.

"What would you like to see done, Paul? Your family has been subjected to Smith's venomous ways, what do you think would put right that wrong?" asked Francis, throwing me the hot potato.

In truth, time had already subdued the hate and vengeance

that I had wanted to inflict on that family. My animal instinct would have been to rip his head off, but I'm simply not a violent person. Converting hate and vengeance into physical action really isn't so easy to carry out in reality.

"I was interested in what you said about the Smiths' fear of doing time. Wild uncontrollable animals should be behind bars. I suppose if I heard that Stephan Smith and his family had been given twenty-five year prison sentences and a recommendation that they served at least twenty years, then I would be satisfied. From what you have said, I believe that incarceration would be pure hell for them."

"And the money?"

"I don't know, Reg. I don't think they should be allowed to keep it."

"I agree."

Francis looked at both of us before continuing. "To hear that the Smiths had received prison sentences of around twenty years and the money confiscated would give me some faith in what that elderly couple's son said in his letter, that 'What goes around, comes around'."

"That won't happen without a bit of help," asserted Reg. I nodded in agreement.

"So what do you suggest, gentlemen?" asked Francis.

The three of us looked across at one another, each waiting for the other to say something. As had become his habit, Reg was the first to break rank.

"I'm a great believer in things happening for a reason. Seizing that opportunity is up to the individual. I have to ask myself whether there is something we could do to see justice done, and possibly make a few bob in the process?" There was a distinctive glint of devilment in Reg's eyes. "Here is a chance for us to snatch control of Smith's life and see how he likes being at someone else's mercy, having to take orders without question and being scared shitless for once in his life."

"What are you suggesting? Kidnapping?" His voice calm and cool, Francis asked the question without altering his manner one way or another. I suppose being an analyst must have had something to do with this impressive ability.

"What I'm saying," Reg went on, "is do we pass this meeting off as a coincidence or for use of a better word 'exploit' it?"

Suddenly I knew in my heart that, coincidence or not, my opportunity had arrived. I had been given a second chance for a father to put things right, to see justice done for the rape of my daughter. My mind flashed back to that Saturday afternoon and then revisited the weeks and months that followed. I had done the right thing by not letting Alison and Charlotte go through the ordeal of a court case. The insight that Francis had shared with us tonight left me in no doubt that my decision had been right. Even so, something inside me was still saying 'The job's not over'.

"You can run, but you can't hide," I muttered.

Reg and Francis looked up at me, trying to work out what had prompted the statement I'd just made.

"It's what Clint Eastwood said," I explained. "Well that's exactly how I've felt for three years. If I hadn't met Reg, and then you Francis, tonight would not have happened. But I did and it has. So what I say is if an opportunity arose to see Stephan Smith and his family pay for the years of hurt and misery they have inflicted on so many innocent people then I would be willing to listen and consider any plan."

Just saying those words made me feel good. While the yoke on my shoulders had not been lifted, it was suddenly feeling much lighter.

"So, is there a plan, Reg?" asked Francis.

"If that's the term, Francis. It's certainly worth looking into. I agree that this is way too much of a coincidence to let it pass by."

There are times in everyone's life when situations and places are so right and so surreal that you wish you could bottle them. That night was a case in point, as I sheltered in the comfort of the farmhouse in the trusted company of Reg and Francis while the rain, wind and thunder flashed and hammered relentlessly.

For three hours we earnestly debated what was the best way to deal with the Smiths. It wasn't the talk of fantasists or drunk men, it was the talk of three ordinary men committed to seeing right win over wrong. Several intelligent and constructive ideas came out of our discussion around the table that night. Francis filled us with the key facts that he knew about the Smiths. Their weakness was their fear of jail; one of their strengths was their unprincipled solicitor. David Buxton had always played an important part in the family's Houdini-like ability of escaping from seemingly impossible situations. I wasn't about to make judgement on their solicitor, but as my old granddad used to say, show me a trade or profession which doesn't have its share of bad apples and I'll show you a milking cow which can give you malt whiskey.

We concluded that kidnapping was the only option open to us, even though Francis had pointed out the seriousness of the crime. Any money received as a ransom, or reward, would be channelled into deserving causes that were most in need of funding. Reg added a proviso that in light of the danger we would be exposing ourselves to we should set aside a safety net for each of us, in case anything went wrong. I had mixed feelings about this at first, as it smacked of profiteering, but Reg's logic was that wherever risk was involved, you always took out insurance to protect yourself. Perhaps he had a point. If I got myself injured or involved in a legal case, then my family and I would need some money to see us through.

Reg had taken in everything that had been said that night and he filled with the enthusiasm and passion of a modern-day Robin Hood. He was the obvious leader for our team. Our plan was almost complete by the time we retired for bed. The only thing that still needed to be thrashed out was how not to get caught. None of us wanted to spend the rest of our lives looking over our shoulder.

That night I listened to Spear and Shake softly breathing as they slept contentedly on their new settee and found myself mesmerised by the dancing flames in the fireplace. As I began to take stock of what I was letting myself in for, I became aware of a real fear. Of course, that was the difference between Francis, Reg and me. Be they a fighter pilot or a cross-dresser, they both had that inner strength and outer confidence to bravely fight their cause. If our plan was to become reality, I needed to find my inner strength, and fast.

"Morning," declared an overbright and breezy voice.

"Morning Reg," I mumbled.

Reg was placing some fresh logs on the fire to warm up the room.

"Did you sleep well?" he enquired.

"Very well, thank you," I replied.

"There are razors, towels and so on in the bathroom down here, but you are welcome to use my ensuite if you prefer," he offered.

"No, that's fine," I said. Within half an hour I was showered, shaved and standing in Reg's conservatory looking at the lines of steam rising from the pine forest below as the heat of the day went to work with nature to make amends for the previous night's downpour. Francis entered, clasping a mug of coffee.

"Beautiful, isn't it?"

"Yes, truly stunning," I agreed.

Francis stood beside me, taking in the picturesque views. I felt I wanted to say something about what we had dared to discuss and plan, but I didn't know where to start. Then, without really thinking about it, I blurted out, "Do you think our lives are mapped out for us?"

"I don't know, Paul. I suppose the only sort of honest answer I can give you is to tell you what I believe in. If I can help somebody as I go along this road then my life is not in vain. An old drag queen, a good friend of mine, used to end her show with that line every time she performed."

I was just about to tell Francis that I agreed with his positive view on life, when Reg appeared holding a large tray laden with croissants, toast, marmalades, jams and butter. He placed it on the table and disappeared, only to return with tea and coffeepots, milk, cream and sugar, and a large jug of freshly squeezed orange juice.

"I'll say this for you Reg, you certainly know how to look after your guests."

I heartily agreed with Francis.

"Now, shall I be mother?" Francis began to pour the tea.

"Well I'd say that you're better qualified than us two!" quipped Reg.

"I'll take that as a compliment," replied Francis with a grin.

As we ate breakfast, a couple of red kites flew over the valley below. Just like the previous evening there was a surrealness, a sense of something right, a feeling that although the three of us were very different in so many ways the camaraderie and trust we had formed in such a short space of time was meant to be.

Five minutes later the pace was cranked up by Reg. Taking up his glasses, pen and notepad, he declared, "Gentlemen, last night I worked on a plan, one that I would now like to put to you. Paul, Francis, do you still stand by what you said last night, that you would seriously consider kidnapping and holding Stephan Smith to ransom to make him accountable for his catalogue of crimes, if a foolproof plan could be put together?

I believe that we have such a plan; however there are two issues we should agree on before this goes any further. First, my plan requires a fourth person. Would either of you object?"

Francis didn't seem too surprised at Reg's request, but I did. I felt comfortable with just the three of us and was reluctant to bring in an outsider.

"Who would the fourth person be? Do you have someone in mind, Reg?" I asked cautiously.

"As a matter of fact, I do, Paul," he replied.

Reg was looking straight at me. "That's the problem too, though, as there's only one person it can be."

He glanced down at the table and then back up at me.

"The fourth person would have to be Otis, your son."

CHAPTER FOUR

"Forget it. there's absolutely no way that I'd let my family get involved," I declared.

My fierce response to the idea that Otis should be the fourth member of our team had clearly taken Reg by surprise. For once he didn't have an immediate answer.

"I apologise, Paul, for being presumptuous," he said.

His apology was genuine. His voice and mannerism conveyed sincerity, but I could still sense Reg's disappointment. He had spent most of last night in the library working out this plan, and now it had fallen at the first hurdle – me.

"More tea and toast, gentlemen?"

"If I've gone up a dress size I'll know who to blame," grumbled Francis.

His comment broke the damp atmosphere created by my outburst.

"More tea and toast would be lovely, Reg, and would you mind if I borrowed a couple of sheets of paper and a pen to jot down some notes?"

"Help yourself, old boy." Reg passed both the book and pen to Francis.

"More tea and toast for you, Paul?"

"Yes please, Reg." I could see it was going to be a long time before lunch if we were going to get this plan sorted.

While Reg busied himself with a second round of breakfast,

I stared out of the window, lost in my thoughts. Francis was frantically writing away. The purposeful stroke of his pen on the paper told me that he was in full flow of something important. I would not be popular if I distracted him by talking right now. As Reg returned, weighed with more toast and a fresh pot of tea, I offered him an apology.

"Sorry for that outburst, mate."

"My insensitivity was to blame, Paul," he replied generously. I am sure that between us we can conjure up another solution that will sort out the Smiths. Now, who is going to be mother this time?"

Instinctively we both looked across to Francis.

I have to admit that the news of his cross-dressing came as a bit of a shock at first, but it didn't take long for me to realise that what he did in his private life in no way changed the fact that he was a really decent bloke. Honesty and humour were his weapons, and words like 'freak' and 'outcast' were terms that I for one would never lay at his door.

Francis now looked up from his notepaper and spoke.

"Paul, with respect, I know why Reg had Otis in mind for our team. With your permission, can I tell you six good reasons why?"

I was intrigued. How could two men who had never met my son be so confident that he was the perfect candidate to be our fourth man?

"With your permission, Paul?"

Francis was looking at me to get the ok to start.

"Ok, but as I said, my son has no involvement."

"I respect that, Paul. Really."

Reg nodded in agreement.

"Like you, I don't know the details of Reg's plan yet, but when he identified Otis as the missing member of our team, I bet this was why. The first three reasons are easy. He's a doctor, a qualified pharmacist and has 12 years' experience in the army."

Reg looked across at me, then back at Francis.

"Fourth reason is that having your son on board would make our team a tight ship – no outsiders; and fifth, you mentioned that Otis is a keen rower and rugby player, which must mean he's still pretty fit."

"Yes, he is," I said proudly. "So what's the sixth reason?"

"There's a bottle of brandy in the cellar with your name on it if you get that one right," teased Reg.

It seemed I was the only one who couldn't see what was blindingly obvious to the others. The previous evening I had shown them a couple of family pictures that I keep in my wallet and on my phone. Both men had taken their time looking at them, and I remembered that Francis had asked a couple of questions about Otis, his age and his specialism as a doctor. I had instantly gone into my proud father routine, relating my son's proficiency in plastic surgery and the reputation he had made for himself in breast reconstruction over the last two years at a clinic in Barcelona. I admit that I thought Francis was hoping Otis might be gay, in which case he was going to be disappointed.

It was Francis that now revealed the elusive sixth reason.

"Reg would have wanted Otis on the team for the simple reason that he looks like Stephan Smith. He could almost be his double with a few slight changes."

The thought that there could be any likeness between the two men made me cringe. The mere sight of Stephan Smith's face had only ever caused me to turn away in disgust. Like it or not, though, I could see what they meant. There was a similarity in their appearance.

"You're both right," I agreed, "Otis does resemble Smith."

I didn't like hearing myself saying it out loud, but it was true. Trouble was, now I wanted to hear the details of Reg's plan, if only to understand how Otis could fit in.

"As I said, Otis is not to be involved, but I'm still interested to hear your plan."

"Me too," said Francis. "It's time to unveil your scheme please Reg. We're all ears."

"I'm glad and relieved to hear it, gentlemen. So let me ask you this. What is the perfect crime?"

Reg paused for a second, then regardless of whether we had a response or not, he carried on.

"Well, I'll tell you. The perfect crime is one that was never committed. My intention was that once we had kidnapped Smith, we would replace him with Otis for three weeks. During those three weeks, Otis, now Stephan Smith, would be out of the country while we held Smith captive. That's the plan in brief. Now let me lay it out for you in more detail."

"Initially, Francis would return to the UK for a month, with a number of jobs for him to complete in that time. He'd need to buy a camper van and a Transit, then find somewhere secure to park them. He'd need to put together some costumes too, although I think it would be safer for me to buy them here. Your main job, Francis, would be to follow Smith, learn his routines, where he goes and who goes with him. Our success depends on this groundwork, you see, because we must get him on his own. Finding that time is going to be the challenge; Smith is all too well aware of sticking to a policy of 'safety in numbers'. Once we've snatched him, we'll take him to a safe house or the camper van and slap a D/D on him."

"What's a D/D?" I asked, looking to Francis for help, but he simply shrugged his shoulders in reply.

Reg, of course, had the answer.

"D/D stands for dynamite diapers. It's is a pair of crotchless boxer shorts that allows you to carry out necessary bodily functions, but is wired with explosive to blow up the wearer. The blast would be enough to remove their most valued possessions, but it would not kill them."

"Which sick madman thought that idea up?" I asked, in disbelief that any human would contemplate doing that to another.

"I did" came the reply. Reg showed no emotion whatsoever, but Francis was clearly struggling to stop himself laughing out loud at Reg's curt response.

"Let me finish, Paul. There will never be any detonation, no explosion and no-one will lose their bollocks. Wherever we finally place Smith in captivity, there will be a TV and DVD player set up. On it we will run a snuff movie showing two men wearing the device and what happens to them when it is remotely detonated. They will then be visited by their captor who will finish them off with a shot to the head."

"Count me out," I said promptly, "we're no better than Smith and his cronies if we go down that route."

"Let me finish, Paul," suggested Reg again politely.

As much as I wanted to walk away from that table, I knew I was obliged to stay and hear him out. I just couldn't accept that the generous and kindly man I had met a week ago was capable of contemplating such horrific crimes against another human being. I swallowed hard and gestured to Reg to continue. He acknowledged with a smile.

"The two people in the snuff movie will be actors."

"Hmm, I must check my equity card is up to date," quipped Francis, unaware that the joke was about to backfire on him.

"That's right, Francis. You and Paul would be the two actors. My intended plan was that no-one would get physically hurt. I give you my word on that. The D/D pants must give the wearer the sensation that something – namely the pack of explosive – is there. Once they are in place and Smith has watched the movie, we'll release him to drive back to his house, fully wired up with a spycam and microphone.

"We'll give him orders to pick up the basics for a trip away, so he'll need a suitcase full of clothes, passport, credit cards and bank account details. He's then to tell his mother and eldest brother that a deal has come up with a Russian businessman that'll give them sole control over any cocaine movement in the south of England. He'll explain that he's going to Brussels and that he's going alone. That's the part that they'll find strange. However, if he explains quietly to his mum that he's met a girl who he hopes might be the one and is taking her as his companion for the trip ... well, what mother is going to stand in the way of a possible wedding? It's not the most plausible alibi in the world, but it was the best I could think of!

"After that, he'll head for Belgium by boat and car. If he

gets stopped at customs, he'll say he's on business. We'll have to provide a good cover for him to make him look like a sales rep, with brochures and letters to support his story and stop any alarm bells from ringing.

"Assuming that he makes it through customs, he'll head for Belgium and stop at the last service station in France, finding a quiet place to park up. This is where the switch will take place."

Reg paused for a few moments to take a sip of tea.

"In my plan, Otis would then become Stephan Smith and carry on the journey in his place. A drugged-to-the-eyeballs Smith would be brought to Spain and imprisoned in one of those cargo containers by the side of the barn. I've drawn up a rough plan of how we could use it."

He pushed forward a sketched outline of a container, buried from view, to serve as a prison cell.

"I'll explain about the cell in more detail later. Let's carry on with the order of events first. Smith will be offered an ultimatum to come in with 'us', a large and powerful Russian drug operation. There'll be two choices: join us or instant death by drowning. The cargo container will contain two taps that are controlled from outside. If he refuses to cooperate, we'll turn the water on and simply leave it running 'till the container's full. Nothing he'll find too difficult for him to understand, I believe. We'll give him an hour to decide and gradually increase the pressure with threats to harm other members of his family until he reaches the right decision. It shouldn't take long for him to make the right choice, given that he stands to make money by cooperating with us."

I wanted to ask what we would do if he surprised us and said

'No', but I didn't want to stop Reg mid-flow. I comforted myself that he had already give his assurance that no-one would die.

"Smith would then start to give instructions to move his money around and to buy in as much coke as possible. They've got plenty of storage space to help them spread it around the South East. He'll have told his family that he'll keep in contact by text rather than by voice, as he'll naturally not want his supposed girlfriend to hear anything she shouldn't. The contact will simply see Smith's name displayed on the phone and so won't have any reason to suspect that it's anyone other than Mr Big himself giving orders."

Reg looked across at Francis for reassurance that his plan was so far on the right track. Nearly the whole of his plan was based on what Francis had told us about Smith the previous evening. I had to confess that up until now the operation seemed reasonably feasible, but that all changed as the next stage was revealed.

"I estimate Smith to be worth about £70 million. This includes money he had accumulated before the lottery win as well as his property portfolio, cars and so on. There'll also be the interest on that money. Assuming that £10 million is tied up in property and goods, let's assume that £60 million is being held in various offshore accounts. My intention is to let Smith order in and stash up as much cocaine as the family can lay its hands on, so that they cause the street price to quadruple overnight."

Again, Reg looked across to Francis for support.

"To finance an operation on this scale, Smith will have to transfer about £40 million to a Swiss bank account, which I'll have set up to the tune of about half a million."

"How much?" Francis and I chimed together.

"You can lay your hands on that sort of money?" I dared to ask.

"Yes," said Reg in a matter-of-fact way. "I've been fortunate in that I've been left a couple of valuable properties in the last few years, plus books are a very lucrative business, don't forget. As well as my library here, I keep a number of books in bank vaults in Barcelona and London. They probably have a total value in the region of £22 million, I'd say."

"So what's your most valuable book kept here?" I had to ask.

"Well, first editions command the highest prices. To give you an idea, there's a dozen or so books that I paid less than £20 apiece for, but if I were to sell them now, they would fetch between three and five grand each."

Much as I wanted to find out more about the value of his library, it was more important to get back to hearing the rest of Reg's plan.

"Otis, alias Stephan Smith, will make himself known to the bank, confirm that the correct contact details are on record, so that there's no danger of the Smith family back home getting wind of the account, and explain that large amounts of money would be moving in and out of the account while he set up his new venture, a furniture business. Discretion and privacy is paramount for banks, so I think we can expect them to stay calm about the amount of activity taking place in the new account. Once the £40 million hits the account, Otis will start to draw the money out in eight transactions over a three-week period. On each occasion, one of us will take the money and deposit it in other bank accounts and safe deposit boxes. At the end of the three weeks Smith will be drugged and driven to Malaga, where the switch back between Stephan and Otis will take place. Smith will come round to find himself in a top-of-the-range hire car with an air ticket to Heathrow to ensure his safe return home. The next day, Stephan Smith and his entourage will be arrested in connection with holding a significant stock of cocaine in various storage facilities across the region."

Reg paused briefly before delivering his final remarks.

"My plan is not one-hundred per cent foolproof. It's got several, what I call, 'hot spots' where we will have to abort the plan or risk being caught. In fact there are seven in total. First, the prison. The problem is how to avoid getting spotted digging out the hole and sinking the container in it. Luckily, visitors up here are rare. On occasions, one of the Romma's will pop in unannounced, but one thing is certain, you'll never see anyone after dark. Therefore, with four of us working from six in the evening to eight the following morning, we would be able to dig out a hole big enough to bury the container and pull the five remaining containers around the back of the barn, something I have wanted to do for ages. This will prevent anyone realising that one has suddenly vanished. With a couple of vehicles, Paul's trailer and my old tractor with the bucket on the front, we should manage the job in a night."

Reg waited to gauge our reaction.

"Personally, I think it's a bit ambitious. Why don't we just hire a JCB and get the job done in next to no time?" I asked.

"Getting a JCB is no problem. The Romma's have got one they would lend me. The trouble is that if we hired one they would be offended and if we borrowed theirs they'd insist on helping us. Good neighbours can be a pain sometimes!"

"I suppose it's not impossible," I said, in an attempt to give

Reg a little support, even though I thought it was a mammoth task with a minimal turnaround time.

"Once the container's in the ground, any other work such as plumbing and electrics can be carried out later. The main thing is to get it in the ground and hidden."

"What's going to happen to it once it's served it purpose?" I asked.

"That's easy and, again, something I've been meaning to do since I moved up here. Along with restoring the barn and making it a library, I intend to convert this barn into an indoor swimming pool, with a mini-gym and bar."

"One question, Reg."

"Yes, Francis?"

"What are we going to do with the earth we dig out?"

"Good point. Dig a hole and bury it, I suggest!"

A bit of humour from Reg was a welcome relief, given that he had been so serious while outlining the plan for the past twenty minutes.

"The only thing that comes to mind is to make a start on that collapsed barn using some of the material to cover over the freshly dug earth. It should work if we don't pile it up too high. Of course, this will also have to be done within the 14 hours."

I couldn't believe it. The mammoth task was still growing, but Francis didn't seem to be concerned. He really was 'Mr Cool' when it came to facing the impossible.

"The second hot spot is the worst. Overcoming it will depend on Francis. His job is to find us the best place to hide Smith when we make the snatch. Hot spot number three is Smith going back to his house unaccompanied. All we can hope is that the constant presence of the D/D and the memory of the snuff movie will keep his mind focussed on the job. The next hot spot is out of our hands. If Customs either side of the Channel get suspicious and decide to strip search him, we will have no choice but to abort. The fifth hotspot is the switch. But as long as we do our homework and make sure we are in a dark secluded area of the services, this shouldn't present a real problem. Our sixth hot spot is at the Spanish border. If we get stopped at Customs we'll just have to say that Smith is the worse for wear after a heavy drinking session and hope that the guards don't want to hang about until he sobers up. The last hot spot is getting Smith from his prison here to Malaga. Again, research is the key to success. We will have to do our homework in choosing the right services area for carrying out the switch. Again, I think that night time will be the best time to do it."

"Well gentlemen, that leaves us with just four things (leaving out the most obvious one for a minute) that need to happen to make our little project a success. First, we must ensure that Stephan Smith and his family are left penniless. Second, we must somehow break the loophole that I believe is and has always been part of the criminal underworld's success. Third, Stephan Smith must experience incarceration for himself. He can't carry on letting someone else do time for him. And finally, hope that a judge finally has the balls to hand out a decent sentence. And that, in a nutshell, is my plan."

"One question, Reg. You haven't mentioned what will happen to the money?"

"That's down to all of us to decide. Myself, I believe that we should all take expenses plus the insurance I mentioned last night. I don't think that's greedy and it's good pay for a job well done."

Put that way, as fair reward for fair work, I was persuaded that Reg was right to claim a 'fee'. "I'm sure there are plenty of ordinary folk who would feel it was a small price to pay to get that scum, Smith, off the streets," I said. "However, Christ only knows how I'd explain away that amount of money to Alison."

"Don't worry," said Reg. "I need someone to oversee the building works on my new library and swimming pool. I had the plans drawn up several years ago and I still intend to go ahead. You could be the site manager, Paul."

Reg had certainly covered all the bases.

"Excellent plan, Reg, but I don't want Otis involved. Imagine if we both got caught. What would Alison do with her husband and son behind bars? If it were just me and things went wrong, I could still rely on Otis to hold things together. With all due respect to you and Francis, I have a wife and two children to consider, whereas you and Francis only have yourselves to care of."

There was a silence for a few moments.

"You're a much better parent than I ever was Paul," confessed Reg.

Well that was news to me. It was the first time that Reg had ever mentioned being married or having children.

"I doubt whether she's on the earth any longer," he added.

Sadness came over Reg's face, reminding me of that famous picture of a clown, where no amount of make-up or frivolity could disguise the sadness within.

"You see, there are more than two people at this table who

have witnessed the horrors of drugs and the likes of the Stephan Smiths of this world peddling their evil wares." Reg bit his bottom lip and looked down at the table. Something in his past had clearly taken its toll, and for once he was finding it very difficult to talk.

"When I was flying, my nickname used to be 'Barbie'."

"That's interesting," said Francis, clearly intrigued that Reg might be a fellow cross dresser.

"Nothing like that, Francis," Reg smiled.

"I was given that name because Elizabeth my daughter, from an early age, collected any and everything to do with Barbie dolls. I must have visited the nearest toy shop to every airport in the world trying to track down new additions for her collection. Elizabeth was my life, as was my wife Davina. My work kept us apart a lot, but I always made it up to both of them when I was at home. Trips out, cinema visits, theme parks and as Elizabeth got older the odd pop concert. Sitting through a Wham concert with three screaming twelve-year old girls is not the most enjoyable way to spend an evening, but the fact is I would do anything to return to those times, anything."

"Elizabeth started to change at about thirteen, which was to be expected, preferring to be with her friends than her mum and dad. It seemed like she only bothered to talk to us when she wanted some money. It was just after her fifteenth birthday and I had been away for two months. When I came back her appearance, attitude and her whole persona had changed. She had met a low life, one Stephan Smith."

"The next two years were hell. She was expelled from school, constantly stealing from shops as well as from us. We never spoke, only argued. The constant rows and stress put a wedge between Davina and me as well. We started to bicker over the most trivial things. Eventually Elizabeth moved out just after her seventeenth birthday and Davina took herself off to spend time with her own family and friends down in Cornwall. Me, I simply threw myself in to my work."

"It all came to a head a couple of months later. It was a Thursday in March and I can remember it as clearly as if it were yesterday. I had a four-day stopover in Singapore out of Heathrow. That morning I had taken my car to the garage for a service and intended to pick it up on my return. A technical problem meant we had a 48-hour stand down, and passengers were transferred to alternative flights. I decided that rather than sitting the time out in some hotel, I would return home and immerse myself in a good book. Taking a taxi I asked the driver to drop me off at the end of the crescent as it was such a lovely spring morning that I fancied the walk.

Elm trees lined the road of large Victorian houses, most of which were almost obscured by large hedges. My own house boasted a drive edged with rhododendrons, almost hiding it. However, they could not camouflage the scruffy white top of a Luton Transit van that was sitting in my drive. I watched from a safe distance as two men came out of my house carrying my television. I had no idea who they were until Elizabeth appeared, making jolly of the situation. The pair went back into the house and emerged carrying most of my music system. I walked up to the drive and firmly told them to put back everything they had taken from my house. I had never seen Stephan Smith before, but I had no doubt that he was one of the men standing in front of me. He defiantly put the stuff into the Transit and told me that if I wanted the stuff back I could get it myself."

"It took just a second for the three years of torment and anger to come flooding out. My fist took out a couple of Smith's front teeth as he reeled backwards and hit his head against the back of the van. Before he could recover, I landed another blow on his nose. The sight of blood sent Elizabeth into a hysterical frenzy and she lunged towards me. I firmly moved her aside and said that I never wanted to see her again. I then walked into my house. The other low life who was now standing halfway up the drive never once posed a problem. Once indoors, I poured myself a large Scotch and drank it down straight. I went upstairs to wash and change. When I came back down, the van and its three occupants had gone, taking most of my material belongings. In truth, they meant nothing compared to what I had really lost that day."

"Two hours and half a bottle of whisky later, the sound of a vehicle on the drive snapped me out of my musings about where I had gone wrong. I expected to see a police car. Instead, the latest model Range Rover was proudly parked there. From behind the net curtains, I watched as the driver of the vehicle leant towards the passenger to give my wife a passionate kiss. They both got out of the car, and he pinched her bottom as they walked to the front door, giggling and laughing like a couple of teenagers. For the second time that day I was about to give someone the shock of their life just by being in my own home. Davina turned to stone when she saw me in the hallway. It took just twenty-one words to deliver my message. 'I'll talk to our solicitor Edward tomorrow. For now, do yourself and lover boy a favour. Get out of my sight'.

"I never saw Elizabeth nor Davina after that day. The divorce went smoothly and she didn't contest what I felt was rightly mine. Something else happened that day. I made the decision to take early retirement. I never flew again, moved over here, restored the house, and built my library, well at least the first part of it. The rest you know. Am I happy? I expected to grow old with the woman I loved, the mother of our child. I expected to see my daughter grow into a young lady, a woman, a mother, have a husband who was good to her and grandchildren which we could both have spoilt. I have been denied that."

Reg paused. This was a man whose dreams and emotions had been knocked sideways. "Well, I expect somewhere in the world the sun is over the yard arm."

Reg got up and went to the kitchen and returned with a bottle of malt whisky and three glasses.

"Just a small one?" he suggested.

"Reg, this plan of yours – let me get something clear."

Francis had taken the chair.

Reg was looking straight at Francis. He didn't have a clue where Francis was going with this, and neither did I for that matter.

"For our plan to become the crime of the century, no-one must know that Stephan Smith spent three weeks in a home-made prison. If that can be achieved and Otis has no involvement with the snatch, then he can't be associated with it, because he will be Stephan Smith."

"What are you saying?"

"Paul, if it could be almost guaranteed that your son would never be implicated in this crime, would you reconsider?"

"That's a ridiculous statement, Francis. As soon as Smith is free, he is going to let the world and its mother know that he has been banged up."

"Yes, but will anyone believe him?"

"His family will."

"But where's the proof going to be? Think about it. Thanks to Otis, as far as the rest of the world is concerned, Stephan Smith has been going about his business of his own free will. There'll be hotel bills, clothes left in hotels and credible sightings, text messages, and don't forget Customs will verify that he has crossed back and forth over borders."

"That's my point. How can you guarantee my son's safety? You say he looks like Stephan Smith, and I agree to a certain extent, but they are no way identical."

"I think we can rely on some of Francis's expertise in that department."

Francis nodded in acknowledgement.

"Well, there is one small point you have overlooked about Otis taking part in this plan."

It was at this point that I created the opportunity that Reg and Francis had been waiting to pounce on.

"How do you know Otis would want to be involved?"

Francis leapt straight in.

"I think he should at least be given the choice. Why don't you make the excuse that you forgot to pick the posts up, or there wasn't enough room on the trailer for all the chicken wire, to come back here with Otis this afternoon? While you're gone, I'll study the media shots of Smith so that I can check Otis out when he comes back with you. If I think your son can't be made to look like a near-perfect copy of Smith then we'll drop the whole idea."

It wasn't clear whether Reg was happy that Francis had drawn a line, but nothing more was said on the matter.

"Let's get you loaded up," suggested Francis.

It took three of us to battle against the overgrowth and pull open the massive doors on the barn. I then proceeded to make a pig's ear of reversing the Land Rover inside to make loading easier. It was a very large barn, and considering its rickety appearance from the outside and the previous night's rainstorm, it was still quite dry inside. There was a hayloft to the left of where the chicken wire and posts were stored, and beyond that was the tractor Reg had mentioned. I recognised it to be an Ebro, only because we had inherited two Ebro when we bought our place; one was just about in working order, the other in bits. When I told Reg, he simply replied that they might come in handy when the four of us started digging. "That'll be when you can convince me that you can turn Otis into a perfect clone of Smith, won't it?" I firmly retorted.

CHAPTER FIVE

THE DRIVE FROM REG'S FARM TO MY HOME took just over an hour. I reckoned I could knock about fifteen minutes off the journey if I didn't have to drop off Reg and Francis to pick up the Land Rover, and allowing for Francis to check his lorry and collect some clothes. Towing the trailer must have slowed me down a bit too. A third of this time was spent navigating the track from Reg's farm to the main road. Nothing could be done there to reduce the journey time. Reg had told us that after a bad storm he would often have to get the old Ebro out to clear boulders off the track.

My interest in trying to work out the precise time of the journey was twofold. If over the next three months our plan hit a problem, I would need to know exactly how long it would take to get from my place to the farm. The journey would also provide the only time that I would have to myself, without my family or newfound friends to interrupt my thoughts, however well intentioned they might be. Time to reflect and contemplate, and on my first journey there was plenty of that to be done.

I have never lied, misled or deceived Alison: I love and respect her. Yet, here I was about to embark on a lying spree of the very highest degree. To be a good liar, you need to be devoid of a conscience and to have a good memory. I could handle the conscience side of things, because what we were doing here was absolutely right, and a little white lie here and there was part of that. As for the good memory, long-term was no problem, but short-term? Three years of trying to speak the local lingo could be my judge and jury there, as my family frequently had to bail me out of my floundering attempts.

My thoughts turned to Otis. If he came on board we would have two liars in the house. Our stories would always need to match up. The one thing in my favour was Reg's smart idea about me working for him. Being away from the house for most of the day would limit the scope for me to put my foot in it, but it was also a very neat way to launder the money coming my way at the end of it all. Before we came to Spain, that sort of money wouldn't have excited me. My monthly wage bills hadn't been far off that figure, but my circumstances had changed considerably since then. We owned our property and paid our bills, and income from the harvest and regular jobs gave us a comfortable lifestyle, but I had to admit that £350,000 would make our lives smoother and save us having to dig into our rainy-day capital.

For the next ten minutes, I idly contemplated what we could spend the money on. A second vehicle would be at the top of my wishlist. Alison and Charlotte always passed comment on a 2007 coupe cabriolet whenever we passed the car salesroom en route to the shops. The car would be useful for Alison's cottage industry – cakemaking. When we were still settling in, we invited some of our new friends for tea and they were completely bowled over by Alison's range of homemade cakes. Word quickly spread and she found herself regularly taking orders for celebration cakes or traditional English cakes. She began to run it as a business, hence the chickens on our land which she decided to invest in when the cost of buying eggs started to make inroads on her modest profits. She and Charlotte used their earnings to buy all the things that apparently us men don't understand. The truth is, I am at my happiest when those two are off clothes shopping, having their hair done or looking in bric-a-brac shops.

The other dream item would be a proper swimming pool. One of the first things we bought in Spain was a large above-ground plastic pool, big enough for us all to clamber in and have a splash around. Filling and emptying it was a bit of a palaver, and not a patch on having the real thing.

After that, restoring the two buildings on our property would easily soak up the rest of the money. I always intended that Charlotte or Otis would move into them one day, but until then we could rent them out as holiday lets.

It occurred to me what a lucky man I was. A loving family, good health and a lifestyle I wished I had started thirty years ago. That I should now contemplate gambling all this away seemed ludicrous. If I could turn back the clock to that morning in the square when I first met Reg, would I have taken his offer of chicken wire?

Then I began to think about that Saturday afternoon when I found my naked daughter, shaking and shivering with blood, make-up and tears running down her face. I could clearly see her curled up in a ball like an animal that had been beaten to within an inch of its life. And then the months that followed watching Alison and Charlotte almost disintegrating.

"Scum, bloody scum," I said out loud.

Francis had held nothing back when telling us what Stephan Smith had done and what he was still capable of doing: the disgusting stuff – mutilations, beatings and worse – that had never come to light because he had been sheltered by the drug fraternity. I pulled up quickly and got out of the car. Three pieces of toast, butter and marmalade, several cups of tea and a malt whisky had just made an unexpected encore. It was no reflection on Reg's ability to make breakfast, it was simply fear. Stephan Smith and his henchmen had got to me. If we were found out by the police, it wouldn't take long for Smith and his family to track us down and wreak revenge on us, Alison and Charlotte included.

When I got back in the motor I was close to heading back to Reg's farm to tell him I wanted out, but the freak set of circumstances that had thrown us together kept ringing in my ears. This was a second chance to avenge my daughter's rape and to see those malicious individuals brought to justice. My mind was now in overdrive trying to get things into perspective. There was only one answer, I reasoned. If the plan went ahead, we would have to kill Stephan Smith. Impossible. If anything had been left in my stomach it would be on my lap by now. The thought of actually killing someone turned my guts over. Besides, Otis had devoted his life to saving people, and there was no way that he would ever consent to such a desperate act.

In truth, I couldn't decide whether what I was intending to do was ethically or morally right. Without knowing it, Otis would be the one who would determine our fate in the end. If Francis decided Otis could safely double as Stephan Smith, and if Otis agreed to be the fourth man, then I would accept his decision as fate.

"You ok, Dad?" asked Otis, as I parked up at home.

"Yes, fine thanks son. Just a bit too much food and wine

last night!" I replied, to cover the true cause of my worries.

Alison and Otis were drinking tea at the old farmhouse table we'd inherited when we bought the house.

"Sit down, love. I'll pour you a cuppa," said Alison, planting a big kiss on my cheek. "I need to watch you after a boys' night out."

My first night out on my own in three years and she is suspicious. What is it with women and their sixth sense that detects the smallest hint of something untoward the minute the man in your life leaves the house? Of course, she was right – but she'd never guess what in a million years … I hoped.

Our kitchen was the hub of our home. It still looked like a traditional farmhouse kitchen oozing character and warmth, while at the same time doubling up as a small-scale cake-making factory. I looked around the kitchen for today's output.

"What, no cakes?" I asked.

"I couldn't sleep last night because you weren't there. I was constantly waking up," explained Alison, "so I started cooking at two this morning. Otis has just this minute arrived back from delivering them!"

"Cheers son," I said gratefully.

Now would be a good time to mention Reg's offer for me to manage the redevelopment of his barns.

"Have you taken anything, Dad?" Otis was still trying to nurse my fake hangover.

"No, I'm feeling a lot better; your mother's tea is doing the trick."

"I can see I won't be letting you out again." Alison's joke gave me the opening I needed.

"Well, it's funny you should say that. Reg has offered me a

very lucrative deal. He's got two very large, dilapidated barns that he wants converted, one to an indoor swimming pool with all the extras, and the other into a library."

"A library?" queried Alison.

I suddenly remembered the books that Reg had loaned me and popped out to retrieve them from the Land Rover. I walked back into the kitchen and placed the books in front of her.

"What lovely books," she exclaimed, "I can't believe their condition."

"Does he have a library already then?" she asked.

I prepared to dig my first hole.

"Yes, you could say that. He wants to extend his current collection and has offered me £150,000 to oversee the job, as a one-off payment. The job could last anything from a year to eighteen months, I reckon. Even after tax we should make about £130,000, which isn't bad going, is it?"

Alison had already told Otis about the stranger in the square.

"That's works out at a pretty decent weekly rate, Dad." Otis was clearly impressed.

"I know. Of course, the first four months will include working at weekends sometimes," I carefully pointed out.

Alison was already working through the family wishlist. "Well, there is the swimming pool we've always wanted, and the convertible…."

At that moment, Charlotte walked into the kitchen, and having half overheard the conversation, demanded, "What's that about a convertible, Mum?"

"Your dad has been offered a contract by Mr Challenger," explained Alison.

"Old blue eyes?"

Where did that come from? I looked over at Alison but Charlotte offered the answer.

"Mum thinks he's attractive, for an old man."

What do you mean 'old man'? He's only six years older than me! Well, Mr Nice Eyes has offered me some work. If I take it, we can afford to build a proper swimming pool and buy a new car."

The look in Charlotte's eyes said it all.

Making sure my third item didn't get overlooked, I added, "and a year or so down the line we can start to rebuild the other farmhouses here."

"Dad, of course you can take the job," declared Charlotte.

"Why! Thank you my dear," I replied flippantly.

"It does sound too good to turn down, Dad." Charlotte didn't want to lose sight of the convertible; she'd already started taking driving lessons and had chosen a colour. "Besides, it'll do you good," she added, patting me on the stomach and giving me a hug.

Alison nodded in agreement. I looked over to Otis.

"I'll do what I can to help out around here a bit more, Dad," he offered.

"Me too," said Charlotte, although I knew from experience to take her offer with a pinch of salt!

"Ok then, I'll take it."

I was excited at the prospect of new work and a little more prosperity. The knowledge that the kidnap of Smith would have to be carried out first quickly sobered me up.

Now that Alison knew about Reg's library she was desperate to join Otis and me on our return journey to the farm. I couldn't think of a decent excuse for not taking her and Charlotte along with us, so I phoned Reg to help me out of my predicament. I needn't have worried. Reg's only concern was being able to provide the additional visitors with a decent meal.

We all set off later that afternoon to visit Reg's place. I had forewarned them about the safari-style ride up the track and they bravely clung on to their seats as we tackled the challenging drive. As we approached the Romma's farmhouse we could see an old man standing in the middle of the road with a large round wicker basket at his feet. It turned out that Reg had rung through to his neighbours to help him out with a few groceries, so that he could cater for his unexpected guests, some of whom were vegetarians. The Romma's could not quite get their head around people who did not eat meat, but they had provided a generous selection of farm-fresh eggs, ripe cheese, salad leaves and a loaf of newly baked bread, adding a bottle of homemade sweet white wine to top things off. In fact everything in that basket had been either grown or made by the family, and that included the basket!

As soon as we stopped to collect the basket, it became clear that the Romma's were not going to miss the opportunity to make the acquaintance of each of us. A selection of family members came from the house to introduce themselves. I could now see the reason for Reg's insistence that the Romma's were kept at a distance from our plan. They were the salt of the earth; good, honest hardworking people and their hospitality was overwhelming.

We eventually returned to the car and made our way up the track to Reg's place. As I had expected, the charm of his property met plenty of approval. What I hadn't been expecting was the next comment from Alison.

"Mm, sex on legs or what?"

"You're right there, Mum," agreed Charlotte.

"Who's that?" they asked together.

For some reason I'd forgotten to mention that Francis would be there. They all knew about the English lorry driver who had been held up by the storm, but they thought that he'd already gone on his way.

"That's Francis, the truck driver," I explained.

"Wow, he's absolutely gorgeous."

For three years Charlotte had shown no interest in boys, and either laughed at or dismissed the subject whenever it came up. I thought her ordeal had put an end to securing any kind of male friendship, so hearing her talk in this way was music to my ears. Francis was coming back from taking Shake and Spear for a walk in the woods. On Reg's advice he had taken a half-cocked shotgun, although the dogs could be relied upon to see off any wild boar. Francis took the gun inside and returned with Reg to greet the visitors. Alison and Charlotte were champing at the bit to be introduced to Francis and exchange greeting kisses, Mediterranean style. Otis shook hands with both Reg and Francis and we all followed Reg into the house. I could see from her expression that Alison was already very impressed with the place. "Just wait till you see the library!" I thought to myself.

Reg had prepared glasses of champagne, which he offered before starting a guided tour of the house. Once they had returned, Reg asked if I would mind helping Francis to fetch the basket of delights that the Romma's had supplied. He was subtly giving me the chance to find out the verdict on Otis.

"Well, Francis, what do you think now that you've met Otis?"

I had got straight to the point as soon as we were out of earshot.

"I'll be honest, Paul. With work on his hair, teeth and eye colour, Otis could easily be made to look the double of Stephan Smith."

"Near perfect then?"

"Absolutely," confirmed Francis. "I've never seen Smith in person, Paul, but I've watched and heard countless video and audio recordings of him, and studied more pictures than I care to remember. In character and mannerisms, Otis and Stephan Smith are like chalk and cheese. They don't sound the same, walk the same and they certainly don't smile or laugh like each other. Your son is a loving and genuine guy. I don't have to tell you what Smith is like. The real question now has got to be, can Otis disguise his whole personality to act like Smith?"

I paused for a moment to take on board what Francis had just said. We carried the provisions into the kitchen and returned to the main room. Reg knew we had not had much time to talk, so he suggested that Alison and Charlotte spent half an hour or so in the library choosing some books to borrow. Alison was delighted, while Charlotte seemed only to have eyes for Francis and wanted to stay behind. It was going to be impossible for us to have a private chat with my daughter around, but Reg the fox knew which way to go. He started to unfold the plans that had been drawn up for the barn conversions.

"Are you happy with these plans, Paul? Can we say they're 'near-perfect'?"

Alison tactfully reminded Charlotte that if she wanted to get the convertible, she needed to give Reg and me some time together to discuss the work that would pay for it. That was enough to persuade Charlotte to make a move.

As far I was concerned, there could only be one answer now. "Yes," I replied.

"So, you are happy for me to go ahead with them?" Reg asked.

It was the strangest thing. I was about to make the biggest decision of my life and yet the only thing that went through my head at that split second was disabled parking bays.

"Yes," I repeated.

At this point, we were standing one to each side of the dining table. I was facing Otis and felt it was up to me to start the ball rolling and let him in on our plan. Trouble was, I had no idea what to say or how to invite an innocent person to become part of a multi-million pound robbery and possible murder. The safest bet was to start at the beginning and explain how we had come together. From telling Otis how Reg and I first met in the square, I moved on to outlining how Francis came to know so much about Stephan Smith and finished by telling him about Reg losing his daughter to drugs. At that point, Reg took over and made it quite clear to Otis that from the outset I hadn't wanted him to be involved. As Reg moved onto explaining our plan in more detail, Otis asked to borrow a pen and paper and started to jot things down. Try as I might to read his scrawl, I had no idea what his notes were about. True to his profession, Otis had that style of handwriting that only fellow doctors, pharmacists and their secretaries can understand. Reg rounded off by repeating that I was against Otis becoming involved, and that it was only because he could be transformed into a near-perfect double of Smith that he was being given the choice of becoming our fourth man. Reg went to a drawer and produced two press cuttings on

Smith. He put the articles in front of Otis, for him to study the pictures.

"Sadly, you're right," he said. "I do seem to have a double, and I have to admit it's not the first time that I've noticed it. When Smith got his lottery win and his picture was plastered all over the papers, I was struck by the uncomfortable similarity straightaway, but there was no way I was going to point it out to anybody."

Francis was right about my son's mannerisms: calm, cool and collected. To be fair, you wouldn't want a surgeon who was operating on you to have anything less than those qualities.

"Let me recap," said Otis, "just to make sure that I'm absolutely clear about this. Your intention is to kidnap Stephan Smith without anyone knowing. While he's in captivity I will masquerade as Smith. His family will be led to believe that he is in cahoots with the Russians to bring off a major drug deal. The authorities will attribute the movement of his money to his new furniture empire. During the three weeks he spends locked up he will be forced to order his family to buy and stash cocaine. Is that just cocaine or any other drug types?"

"Any drug, the harder the better," replied Reg, "as it will increase the price of the drugs on the street."

"On his release and return to England, Smith will be implicated and arrested for being involved in the multi-million pound stash of drugs that his family have put in storage. I could not expect to be involved in the most dangerous part of the plan, the snatch." He broke off to look down at his notepad.

"And finally, the £40 million. Has a decision been reached on which charity would receive the money?"

"No," replied Reg.

"In that case, would anyone mind if I chose the charities?" asked Otis.

We all shook our heads in response.

"Well, given the facts. . . ." Before Otis could reveal whether he was in or out, I jumped in.

"Something needs to be said about Otis and me taking part in your plan, Reg. In the event that there is even a small chance of us getting captured, we have to kill Smith. There's no question about that, because if we don't remove him, getting caught by the police will be the least of our problems. The kind of reprisals and revenge that Smith would hand out to our family and friends would be merciless. There is no way that Smith can be allowed to live if he gets any inkling who was or is behind his abduction."

"Point taken, Paul," replied Reg.

"No problem," added Francis. "The same from me," said Otis, "and yes, I do want in."

"Well, that make four," said Reg. "Paddy will be pleased."

Before I had a chance to ask who Paddy was, Alison and Charlotte came back into the room.

"What's this?" asked Alison at the sight of all shaking hands. The fox took up his role once more.

"The new library will contain seven thousand medical books," announced Reg. Otis has just pledged his support once the library is built to help me catalogue and categorise them. We've gone through all the plans and have agreed they are workable."

"That's fantastic news." Alison wouldn't have been so thrilled if she had known the real reason behind the handshakes. She held up the handful of books she had chosen from the library shelves. "If I had a shopping trolley I could fill it ten times over! Your library's a dangerous place, Reg!"

"You're more than welcome," he replied, clearly flattered. "A book is meant to be read as well as collected."

"Would you like to see the books I chose, Francis?" Charlotte sat down on one of the sofas and beckoned to Francis to join her.

Alison offered to help Reg prepare a meal, which left Otis and me to load up the posts and chicken wire.

"Are you shocked?" I asked him as soon as we were outside.

"I suppose I am a bit. I'd never have thought that you would consider getting involved with something as dangerous as this. On the other hand, given the unique set of circumstances that have brought you together, if you had done nothing, you would have spent the rest of your life wondering 'what if'."

We walked over to the barn and pulled the two massive doors open. The resilient grass and undergrowth that had been flattened only a few hours earlier had already started to bounce back.

"Reg is right, sinking one of those shipping containers in here won't be a problem," said Otis. "It's massive. I wonder what it was originally used for?"

"According to Reg, it was always a working farm. Trouble was, the family got smaller and smaller until no-one was left to carry on."

"Shall I reverse in, Dad?" Otis knew I was useless at reversing with a trailer.

"Here you go." Otis handed me a pair of gloves. "You'll need them for handling the wire and wood. The splinters and cuts can play havoc with your hands."

"Oh look, Dad," he said, pointing an object in the corner, "There's a bucketful of staples."

"Yeah, Reg said I could have those too."

"That'll save us some money."

It was unbelievable. We had just decided to embark on a mission to steal millions, yet here was my son advising me to steer clear of splinters and save a few quid. Sometimes I wondered who was the parent and who was the child when Otis was around!

"Good to see Charlotte getting on with Francis," said Otis, who was all too aware how hard she found it to relax in male company.

"Francis is gay, son."

Otis stopped loading the posts and leant on the side of the trailer.

"I find that very hard to believe, Dad. What makes you so sure?"

"It may be that I've only known Francis for twenty-four hours, but he's quite open about his private life."

"I agree that he's a good guy, Dad, all I'm saying is that he does not come across as gay. If I were a gambling man I'd have had a hundred to one that Francis only had eyes for women."

"Well, son, I put my shirt on it that he is, in fact I will put my whole wardrobe."

Otis shook his head in disbelief, and I decided to change the subject.

"I have a question for you. Who's Paddy?"

Otis was still leaning against the trailer.

"Paddy Mann, of course. He would have been any soldier's first choice to have next to him during World War II. He was the founding father of the SAS and his ideas are still used today."

"Four SAS men would come in handy right now," I said wistfully.

"I know, but as things stand we're going to have to cope with three second-hand ones in good condition and one new recruit."

It took a few seconds for the penny to drop. "Hold on, you couldn't have been in the SAS, you're a doctor," I said.

"I was a soldier first, Dad."

"I'm confused. How can you be a fully paid trained killer one day and a passionate saver of lives at the same time?"

"But saving lives is what it's all about, Dad. I will give you an example."

Otis looked down into the trailer for a few seconds, then back at me.

"Take what we intend doing Dad, eliminating Smith and his family by putting them behind bars. It would be better to kill him, because it's well known that he'll still be able to carry on his business behind prison walls. Honestly Dad, it's drug-dealing that will destroy the human race.

"You remember my last five years in the army, spending a couple of months at different hospitals across the country? This was to learn more about the hands-on approach in different fields of the NHS, but it was also to help ease the staffing crisis within the NHS. Up in Manchester, I was posted to the A & E department for a three-month stint. Not my favourite experience, I have to say," admitted Otis with a smile.

"I thought I had seen it all, Dad – in Africa, Bosnia, Iraq – but none of them compared to what I witnessed on Saturday nights in A & E. One weekend we had exceptionally hot weather and the ward was virtually full to capacity. There had been barbecue accidents, heat exhaustion, road-rage victims, and even fingers trapped in sun-loungers. It had just gone 11pm when an emergency meeting was called to warn us that, along with seven other hospitals in the area, we had been put on emergency status. This only happens when there's been a major incident, like a traffic pile up, train crash or terrorist attack, but the cause of our emergency wasn't any of these." Otis paused.

"What we were about to experience was an influx of kids who had been poisoned with illegal drugs at a rave. Within half an hour every off-duty doctor, nurse and porter had been called in to the hospital. It's at times like this, Dad, that you witness people at their best. They were pulling out all the stops to help the naive victims of those money-grabbing bastards who have no respect for human life. In most cases a carefully controlled amount of water and fresh air is what is recommended: on that stinking hot night, they were the two things that were in short supply."

"Just after midnight, the kids started arriving, first in ambulances, then police cars and vans, and even taxis and private cars. The seats in A & E started to fill up. As quickly as the porter found chairs, the kids were filling them. Inevitably it wasn't long before we had our first fatality of the night: an eighteen-year-old girl who was simply beyond help. An hour later, her sister was brought in, resuscitated and placed on a life-support machine. If she survived, brain damage was inevitable. I got the unenviable task of telling the parents what no parent ever wants to hear. The uncontrollable grief of that couple will stay with me as long as I live. Who would want to bring that on anyone and why, for God's sake?"

A tear had formed in the corner of his eye and was now

running down his cheek.

"I'll tell you why, Dad. So some mindless piece of scum can make money from pumping drugs into the veins of kids."

I'd never seen Otis so angry before.

I now remembered reading about this disaster; it was headline news at the time because it was later discovered that a 'free' drug cocktail had been included in the £50-a-head entrance fee. I'd no idea that Otis had witnessed the fallout at first hand.

"Of course, no-one was ever charged or convicted for that night."

"As always," I muttered. "I wouldn't put it past the Smith family to have been connected in some way."

"Whether it was the Smiths or not, all drug dealers are tarred with the same brush as far as I'm concerned," continued Otis. "Until we legalise drugs in this country, we will never be free of this illegal trade."

"Did I just hear you right, Otis?" You think drugs should be legalised?"

"That's right, Dad."

"You got a good reason for saying that?" I asked, puzzled.

"At least those two teenage girls would be alive and well today if drugs had been legal," he replied.

To say I was confused was an understatement.

At this point we heard footsteps. It was Reg coming to check on our progress.

"How are you getting on?" he enquired.

"We were fine until a minute ago when Otis bowled me a googly," I said.

"I told Dad that I believe all illegal drugs should be made legal," explained Otis.

"Damn right," agreed Reg.

"Er, have I missed something here? Two clever and educated men agree on making drugs accessible to all? Explain please."

"They should be legalised, Paul," said Reg in his straight-talking, no-holds-barred way. "I read just a few days ago that if revenue were collected on all the illegal drugs sold through Britain it would match the total revenue amassed from alcohol and cigarettes put together. So I say tax it. Drug-related crime already costs our economy £13 billion a year — it's time we got some reimbursement."

I shook my head in disbelief.

"Paul, ask yourself one question. If your son or daughter had gone down that road as so many kids do, buying and using drugs, would you have preferred them to use, let's say a recognised chemist as their supplier or some grubby, amoral pusher on the street corner who has no qualms about bumping up the quantities with fake or dirty ingredients?"

I looked at Otis for his contribution.

"Dad, we will never stop people from taking drugs What we can do is clean up the dirty, degrading side of drugs and cut out the people who push them."

Reg returned with more justification. "Look, Paul, if a chemist sold them you would know that the drugs were clean and to a high standard. As legalised goods, drugs could be better regulated in terms of who gets their hands on them and the revenue generated from their sale could be used towards educating youngsters down a different route. You've got to remember that one-third of crime in this country is drugs-related. Don't you think it's time we deprived the underworld of its most profitable industry?"

I'm pretty sure alcohol was a contributor to Reg's 'one-third of crime' statistic, but I wasn't about to go there while he was in the mood for fighting talk.

"Ok, you may have a point, but can we agree to disagree for now?" I conceded. I was conscious that we needed to get back to the house before Alison came looking for us.

On our way back to join the others, Reg suggested that we meet the next morning to finalise a few details before Francis headed back to the UK in the afternoon.

"No problem for me," said Otis, "We can be here early, can't we Dad?"

"Of course," I agreed. "And sorry about bringing the girls along today, Reg. I couldn't find a way to get out of it."

"Don't be so bloody silly. This old house hasn't had so much female laughter in years," Reg replied.

After an excellent dinner, we thanked Reg for his hospitality and said our goodbyes. Otis drove us home, while Alison and Charlotte sat in the back and chatted and giggled about their evening. They had clearly enjoyed Francis' good company and conversation. I loved hearing them so happy, but, in my half-drunk state, felt it was only right that I shatter any illusions they might have about his preferences.

"I think you should know that Francis, while a nice guy, is gay," I blurted out clumsily.

"Don't be so stupid, Paul," retorted Alison.

"Yes, Dad, you're way out of line there," Charlotte said, backing her up.

"But Francis wears women's clothes," I protested.

"Tell us something we didn't know!" replied Charlotte.

"We've already agreed to go to Playa de Aro when he comes back, to spend the day shopping with the rich and famous," added Alison.

"Honestly Dad. Just because someone likes to dress up and make themself look attractive doesn't make them gay!" scolded Charlotte.

I could see from the grin on his face that Otis was highly amused at the dressing down I was getting. He decided to join in the fun. "And you know what they say, Dad. Marry a cross-dresser and double your wardrobe!"

Otis and I left just after eight the next morning, making the excuse that we had to collect the last of the posts and chicken wire. We spent most of the journey talking about the plan in more detail. Otis was concerned about how Reg intended the snatch to work. He was right – this was the one part of Reg's plan that still needed to be ironed out.

We arrived to the welcoming sight of freshly made coffee, toast and croissants, and got straight down to business. I started the ball rolling by asking Reg to tell us how the snatch was going to work.

Reg took off his glasses and rubbed his eyes. "In truth, gentlemen, I don't know. What is for certain, though, is that Smith has to be abducted without anyone knowing. Got any ideas, Francis?"

All eyes turned towards Francis; he knew more about Smith than any of us.

"I admit that I've been a bit anxious about this part of the plan. I decided not to mention it until we knew Otis was on board. Here's where I've got to in finding a solution, though. It's based on three key issues: one is that we mustn't kid ourselves that we're abducting some scared old businessman or six-stone weakling. Stephan Smith has a reputation for not giving in. He certainly won't come willingly, so force will have to be used. Two, Stephan Smith is never alone. Whether its family, so-called friends, hangers-on or podders, he makes sure he's always got company with him. Three, as Reg said, no-one must know that he's been taken. In fact, if the plan works, not even Smith will know if he has been abducted or not!"

That last comment raised a chuckle from the team.

"Your suggestions then, please," said Reg, volleying the ball firmly back to Francis.

"There's only one line we can pursue and that is to find a rare thirty minutes in the life of Stephan Smith when he is completely alone. To do that, we need to spend two to three weeks carrying out surveillance. Based on that, we can then plan which road we go down."

Francis looked at the three of us for approval, and found it.

Moving on, Reg said that we needed to decide on a code name that we could use instead of using 'the plan' all the time. "I touched on this yesterday. Has anyone got any suggestions? Something quite simple would be best."

"How about HOLI?" I suggested, having given the matter some thought as I lay in bed the night before.

"I'm happy to go with it," said Reg, "but why HOLI, out of interest?"

"Well, I was trying to find a code name that we can't be connected with, yet a word that would mean something to us all without being too obvious or difficult to remember. I steered clear of names and started playing around with words that were associated with our jobs and interests. Otis, you've been a pharmacist, Francis, a policeman, I was a plumber and Reg, you were a pilot. By taking the second letter from each of these I ended up with HOLI!"

The simplicity of the explanation raised smiles around the table. It was agreed: the plan finally had a name.

CHAPTER SIX

SURVEILLANCE AND OBSERVATION were second nature to Francis: his experience and training was going to be invaluable for HOLI. Before heading back to the UK, he joked with us that not only did he enjoy dressing as a bird, but he was also passionate about watching them – the feathered variety, that is. It was a hobby that he'd started as a boy, spending hours perched in trees or crouched in a hide beside lakes and rivers, trying to take the perfect picture of visiting birds. Now his twitching habit was going to provide the perfect cover for his surveillance duties.

Francis returned his lorry to the depot and informed the agents that he wouldn't be available for the foreseeable future. Next he needed to hire a box van to transfer his possessions from his parents' house and put them in storage. He didn't have any furniture, but he did have a department store's worth of clothes and a shoe collection that Imelda Marcos would die for. He decided to set up camp at a caravan and campsite in Henley-on-Thames, which was far enough away from Smith's headquarters not to cause suspicion and yet close enough to get to and from it on a daily basis.

Choosing a suitable motorhome kept Francis busy, scouring the dealer websites for a day or two before he came across a couple of real possibilities at a showroom in Maidstone. To serve its purpose, the vehicle had to be large enough for him to live in comfortably, agile enough for use in the snatch, and robust enough to make the journey up to Reg's farm. On the forecourt, Francis inspected the two possibilities. One was a newish model with 4,000 miles on the clock and the other was slightly older with 15,000 miles racked up. On the basis that HOLI couldn't afford to encounter problems with wear and tear while trying to make a getaway with Smith on board, Francis opted for the younger model that still had plenty of mileage left in it.

The campsite was virtually empty when Francis booked in. He spent most of the day setting up, then drove into town for some local maps that would show useful footpaths and bridleways leading to and around the Smith property. He was pleased to see that a number of routes ran right past the home which would give him, posing as a rambler, legitimate reason for being so close to the house. Armed with his maps, all that he needed now were boots, beard and bobble hat to complete the look!

At nine the next morning, Francis drove to St Mary's hospital and parked his car. It was a two-mile walk from there to Smith's place, and provided a handy starting point for his daily surveillance duties. Within forty-five minutes he was standing on the ridgeway looking down at Smith's house. It was clear why the property had earned itself the nickname the 'countryside supermarket'. It was as if someone had picked up an out-of-town shopping unit and plonked it straight in the middle of a field. Originally built by a wealthy foreign investor who then got bored with the project, the property was snapped up by Stephan Smith after his lottery win. Since then he had added an eight-car garage with self-contained flat, extended the indoor swimming pool, and put dog kennels and a track at the back of the house. The whole thing looked hideous and tacky. From his viewpoint, Francis could make out the footpath that looked over the front of the property. It made an excellent surveillance post. The only trouble was that it provided a good vantage point for both parties. He scoured the map for other possibilities and came across a small area of woodland named Oak Tree Wood. It lay about a third of a mile away, to the left of Smith's supermarket, and looked like it would make a good hide. From the police reports he had read, Francis knew that previous raids had often failed because they had been spotted by the family before they could reach the property. This gave the Smith residents the opportunity to make themselves scarce or cover up before the police arrived. It seemed the location of the place served the family well both as hideaway and lookout.

There was no obvious reason how the woodland had earned its name, as it seemed to be the exclusive home of well-matured evergreens! Francis worked his way through the trees until he came to an area that overlooked the valley, including the roof and chimneystack of Smith's mansion. The way the land rose and fell at this point obscured a clear view through the valley, but by standing on the second rung of a boundary fence, Francis could see a lot more of the house. He looked around for some elevation and caught sight of a large oak branch singlehandedly pushing aside the neighbouring evergreens. "Must be going soft in the head," he muttered to himself, "but I reckon that branch is beckoning me on!" He duly followed the branch back through the woods to trace its roots, and eventually found its broad trunk firmly standing at the centre point. It was truly the grandfather of the woods. More importantly, the higher branches provided the exact lookout point that Francis had been searching for. However, it was going to take a good length of rope to get him up to the crow's nest. Francis decided to return the next day.

By eight o'clock the following morning, Francis was sitting comfortably aloft in the oak, looking down the valley through his binoculars at Smith's empire. He had trimmed back any evergreen fern that obscured his view and was armed with a small saw to remove any more determined branches that decided to get in his way. As well as a good supply of food rations, he had brought with him a rope ladder, camera, notepad and torch. He was ready to start his daily fourteen-hour surveillance for real.

Francis had just poured his second cup of coffee of the day when he noticed some movement at the property. A woman in her late twenties dressed in a white tracksuit, anorak and trainers appeared on the gravel drive. She was drawing on a cigarette and puffing out smoke at an impressive rate. As three children emerged from the house, her coarse and overloud voice shattered the silence of the surrounding countryside. From what Francis could decipher, her command of the English language needed some serious improvement. As the children shuffled into a car, she swiped the last of the frost off the windscreen and threw herself into the driver's seat. She revved up the engine and headed for the electric gates which obligingly opened just in time for the car to roar through. "Late for school again," Francis thought to himself.

The next time he had the chance to grab a cup of coffee was gone one o'clock. Since his first sighting, traffic movement at the Smiths had kept up a steady pace. Francis had two notebooks, one to log activity and the other to record any bird sightings.

The score was currently one-nil to the Smiths, as the birds hadn't had a look-in all morning. At around eight that evening, Francis decided to call it a day. Hungry and mentally exhausted, he climbed down from his watchtower and headed back to camp, taking stock of the day's events on his way. He could confirm that Stephan Smith had been there. He only saw him briefly when he came out of the front door with his brother Ricky to speak to two podders. With so many security staff, guard dogs and visitors around the place though, it was already clear that snatching Stephan Smith from within the grounds was a definite no-no. Reg wasn't going to be pleased to hear that.

Driving back to the campsite, Francis contemplated what it would take to change popular opinion about the whole drug culture. Given that only ten per cent of drugs and drug dealers are ever seized or caught, it seemed to him that the police had completely lost control of the situation. So what was the alternative? Francis recalled from dossiers he'd studied that three small-scale raids on the Smiths' property had only ever found a small amount of cocaine and grass, despite frequent deliveries and collections being recorded on a daily basis. After the last raid the police had exhausted their financial and legal wherewithal to pursue the Smiths. Until they could get their hands on a concrete piece of evidence, they had to concede the longstanding game of cat and mouse to their sly opponents.

Like any other large-scale dealers, the Smiths took full advantage of their upper hand. The police simply didn't have the time or manpower to tackle this crime head-on and get a noose around its neck. Francis suddenly found his thoughts echoing the argument earnestly put forward by Otis; it was time to think outside the box. If the law was ever going to get a handle on the drugs trade, then making drugs legal could provide a real solution. "Crikey, he's right!" Francis found himself reeling at his sudden realisation. "I never thought I'd find myself going down that route, but suddenly it looks a bloody good idea!"

The second day of Smith-watching showed pretty much the same amount of activity. A succession of lorries, taxis and motorbikes came and went throughout the day. Stephan Smith eventually left just after half-past six, accompanied by a brother and two cousins, plus an entourage of podders and girls. From their loud conversations, it seemed that they were heading for an evening at the dog races. This was supported by the fact that, two hours previously, Francis had watched a couple of trainers gather together about ten greyhounds and put them in a trailer. They had then driven off, presumably to the track to get ready for the event. There was no way that this kind of trip would give HOLI the opportunity to snatch Smith. Reg's plan centred on the team getting hold of him without anybody knowing or suspecting what had happened. Francis was beginning to get concerned that so much muscle and so many hangers-on seemed to follow Smith's every move, 24-7.

It took an extra effort and a very large mug of coffee for Francis to get started the next day. The grass was still white with frost, and the chill wind tirelessly slapped at his cheeks without mercy. Once at the lookout, Smith's supermarket was showing all the signs of it being just another day of traffic to-ing and fro-ing in its anonymous way. About mid-morning, Smith appeared at the front door with a number of family members. They headed towards the back of the house, where they split up. Two walked over to the kennels, while the others made their way to the centre of the practice track. They were all warmly wrapped in long jackets and between them displayed a colourful assortment of baseball caps – essential headwear for chavs! A few minutes later, one of the handlers approached the track, leading two greyhounds which looked pitifully cold without their fleeces on. "Surely they'd need those on today," thought Francis, "I can see them quivering from here." Suddenly, from the other end of the kennel, the two men appeared again, one with a pair of Rhodesian ridgebacks and one with a pair of American pitbulls. Francis was pretty sure that it was Smith's brother, Rick, and his cousin Allan. All four dogs were straining at the collars, clearly testing the strength of the men who were struggling to keep control. Francis didn't like the look of the dogs, nor did he have a good feeling about what was going to happen. "Surely not that..." he gasped.

You can normally categorise violent criminals as either mad or bad: Rick and Allan had both traits in abundance. Smith's appetite for blood sports was well-known. Dog fighting, badger baiting and coursing were as normal to him as watching a game of football or cricket. The two greyhounds, whose only fault was to come third and fourth in their races the previous evening, were to pay for their failure. Before instructing the handler to let the first greyhound off its lead, Stephan Smith walked up casually to the dog and kicked the poor animal in the stomach, a sure way to slow the animal down. From there on it didn't have a chance against the cannonball instincts of the ridgebacks. Wounded and confused, the greyhound ran to the far corner of the track for safety. It stood there shaking, awaiting its fate, making cries and yelps that filled the silent, cold air. The ordeal took just over a minute. Stunned by the appalling act of inhumanity, Francis felt sick with disgust at the nonchalance and arrogance of each and every one of the people standing on that track as they watched the second dog meet its end.

That evening, as Francis recounted to Reg by phone what he had seen, he volunteered that if operation HOLI couldn't be put into place, he would willingly assassinate Stephan Smith himself.

I wasn't proud of it, but when I heard this my immediate reaction was that if it came to assassination, my part in HOLI would be over with and I'd no longer be involved. I felt a coward and a cheat for being this way, but my growing nervousness was eating me up. If only you could bottle anger and hate and then pour it out at will. I needed to remain focussed on why I'd agreed to be a member of the team. I was there to avenge the rape of my daughter and the near-destruction of my family, pure and simple. There were so many positive outcomes to be gained from Reg's master plan, that I had a duty to think positive and stay the course for everyone's sake.

By Sunday morning, winter had declared itself. It was a cold, crisp day, the sort when you take a deep breath and almost stop breathing. Perched in his lookout and thankful for his thermals, Francis watched a pair of muntjacs foraging for food at the foot of the mighty oak. Several horseboxes and trailers came and went down Wardrobe Lane, heading for the large equestrian centre in the village. Francis couldn't understand why they even attempted to negotiate the lane when, if they stayed on the main road for another mile, they would come across a large sign with an arrow showing the most direct and easiest route. It was now a quarter to ten, and apart from two Dobermans wandering around the front yard, all was quiet at Smith's supermarket. For a brief moment, Francis wondered whether the Smiths had taken themselves off to church!

Suddenly both Dobermans turned their attention to the front door as it flew open to reveal Stephan Smith, no less, with no-one else around him. Smith strutted over to his car, opened the back door and both dogs jumped straight in. Getting into the driver's seat, he started up the engine and drove off via Wardrobe Lane. All this took less than a minute. The sight of Smith on his own took Francis aback. He desperately wanted to phone Reg on the spot to tell him the news, but knew it was pointless until he had gathered more information.

Twenty minutes later Smith returned, flinging an empty can out of his window as the car drew to an abrupt halt. He let out the dogs and a large belch, grabbed a handful of newspapers and returned to the house. Was the newspaper run a one-off or a weekly Sunday morning event? Both the dogs acted as if it were a regular occurrence.

Francis decided that his next move should be to find where Smith had bought the papers and make some discreet enquiries. He already had a good idea where to go. There was a parade of shops about a mile and a half away on the main road heading towards Slough; Smith could easily have made the round trip there in that time. He decided to leave surveillance for the day and headed to his storage locker for a change of clothes. Transforming yourself as a man to look like and take on the character of a woman is one thing, but to carry it off to perfection is a fine art. As he drove to the storage depot, Francis mulled over which of his 'women' would be the best for the job. He decided that a reporter from the local newspaper doing a piece for a magazine on lottery winners would be the best choice. He didn't have any idea where Smith had bought his winning lottery ticket, but this at least would be a feasible ploy for getting the newsagent to open up.

Later that afternoon, Francis was standing outside a small minimart in a parade of shops, taking a quick glance at his reflection in the shop window to check that he looked the part. Dressed for winter in a beige duffel coat, roll-neck sweater, calf-length skirt and Ugg boots, Francis entered the shop and wandered along the aisles. There was only one other shopper to be seen, an old girl at the far end looking through birthday cards. He approached the smiling Asian couple behind the counter who welcomed him as if he were a longstanding customer. He asked for two bottles of Scotch and a handful of scratch cards which, he hoped, would persuade them that he was worth talking to. While the wife rang the goods up on the till, the husband carefully wrapped up the bottles and handed the lottery cards to Francis, wishing him the best of luck. This gave Francis the inroad he was looking for.

"Actually I was wondering if you could help me with that. I'm doing an article for a magazine at the moment, all about lottery winners. Someone told me that Stephan Smith, the man who won millions on the Euro lottery, bought his ticket here." Just the mention of that name wiped the smiles from their faces, and they shook their heads earnestly.

"No, no, you must be mistaken," replied the man nervously.

His wife muttered something quietly in Punjabi to him, little knowing that Francis could understand the gist of the language thanks to a childhood friendship with a boy called Mohammed from north-west Pakistan. Going round to play at Mohammed's house after school, Francis had found that Punjabi was the only language spoken by his friend's family and had gradually picked up a good understanding of what was being said. "Just tell her that he didn't buy the winning ticket here and don't mention that he comes here on Sundays," she warned.

"My wife says he's a nice man who we see passing by now and then, that's all" lied the man feebly.

That was all the confirmation Francis needed to be certain that Stephan Smith made a weekly run for the papers. He'd need to keep up his surveillance over the next two weekends to be absolutely sure, but he reckoned he finally had the news that Reg wanted to hear. Operation HOLI was on.

CHAPTER SEVEN

AS FAR AS WE WERE CONCERNED, our best opportunity to snatch Smith was going to be on his Sunday morning newspaper run. Quite rightly, Francis felt that we were being a little premature in putting all our eggs in one basket at this point. Stephan Smith had only ventured outside his front gate twice in one week, and on both occasions it was a night-time excursion to the dog races. He was clearly a nocturnal creature, so Francis decided to change his surveillance time to six in the evening through to six in the morning to see if any other opportunities presented themselves.

Back in his lookout post, Francis endured a severe change in the weather, with torrential downpours on both the Monday and Tuesday nights. On both nights a black Chevrolet was taken out by Rick and Allan Smith with a couple of sidekicks also on board. It didn't return until at least five in the morning, and Francis felt he could safely conclude that it was used as a 'passion wagon' throughout the night. Just to test his theory, he decided to use one of his female aliases to find out more. The next evening, Caroline emerged from Francis' wardrobe, dressed in a black leather knee-length dress, black tights, heels and an ash-blonde wig. She waited in a snack-trailer lay-by en route from the Smith property to any of the likely destinations, London, Slough, or the motorway, but the evening proved fruitless. The lads had obviously been in need of a night in to catch up on lost sleep.

By Friday, Francis decided it was time to treat Caroline to a return visit to the lay-by. There were three or four other cars and half a dozen lorries when she arrived at eight. It wasn't until an hour or so later that the passion wagon drove past. Rick Smith was in the passenger seat, but Caroline couldn't make out any other faces because of the blackened windows. She pulled out and followed the van at a safe distance all the way into London.

As the traffic got heavier, she found it harder to keep on the tail of the Chevy as it headed through Hammersmith and on towards Chelsea. At South Ken, the traffic lights went against her and Caroline thought she had lost them for good. A lucky turn into one of the side streets brought the Chevy back into view, where she smiled to see it stuck behind a learner driver who had stalled. The frantic pounding of the horn suggested that Smith and his cronies were right out of patience. Once on the move again, the wagon turned off down another side street and pulled up outside a night club where two huge bouncers stood guarding the canopied entrance. Caroline parked further up the road and watched from her rear-view mirror. Someone got out of the wagon and was escorted into the club by a bouncer as though he was a celebrity. Ten minutes later he returned and got back inside the wagon, exchanging a quick chat and a laugh with the bouncer before the Chevy roared off.

Keeping a careful tail on the wagon for the next three hours, Caroline watched as the same routine was repeated across town. The Chevy would stop; the same man would get out, enter a club and return after ten minutes. They were always expected, with a line of cones placed in the road for them to park and bouncers waiting to show them in. It was blatantly obvious that this was a delivery run to feed the drug-hungry punters in need of a high that would take them into the weekend. What puzzled Caroline was why they didn't make more of an effort to cover their tracks. Wouldn't you park at a distance rather than slap-bang in front of the club? Or vary which of them made the delivery? Why would you take such risks? It just didn't add up.

By 3.30am, the wagon appeared to have completed its run and started to head back home via the M4. A thick fog had built up and Caroline was finding it difficult to keep the tail lights in view, let alone the rest of the vehicle. The indicators started to flash as they turned into the services. Caroline assumed they were going to refuel. The wagon pulled up outside the service station and staked its claim on the disabled parking bay. Caroline pulled up behind an island of shrubs and watched the four men make their way across the footbridge to the cafe. She had the advantage of being able to follow their movements through the well-lit building, whereas they could see nothing through the black and foggy night. However, what she couldn't see was a sign on the cafe indicating that it didn't begin serving food until five o'clock.

Compromising oneself is something you are taught about as a soldier in the SAS – how to avoid it, and how to get out of it if you find yourself in that position. After more than six hours in the car, Caroline needed to powder her nose, so to speak. Armed with her handbag and umbrella, she checked the lobby was clear before heading for the ladies.

Emerging from her comfort stop, she caught sight of two figures standing outside. It was Allan and Ricky Smith. She quickly dived behind one of the arcade games in the lobby and waited for the men to move on. Too late. A pair of lecherous eyes had spotted her. "What have we got here?" said a voice that sent a shiver through her whole body. For a few minutes, Francis experienced the fear and terror that strikes a woman faced with the threat of being raped. Caroline was now trapped between Allan and Ricky in the lobby and their two sidekicks loitering outside the entrance. Running wasn't an option – high heels saw to that, besides, where could she run to? Nor was Caroline prepared to blow her cover, so that left just one option.

"Is that slag with anyone?" asked Ricky Smith.

Both men were looking Caroline up and down like a piece of meat hanging in an abattoir.

There was no question what Allan was thinking: mercy or consequences were the last thing on his mind. "I've got a surprise for you, you posh slag," he sneered.

Seeing what Allan was building up to, the other two men opened the entrance doors to smooth his exit from the lobby. Ricky gestured towards the cameras, "Get the slag outside."

Caroline found herself shoved towards the doors by one of the heavies. "Fucking move," he snarled.

Being caught on camera wouldn't have done Caroline any favours. The last thing she needed was exposure, so she obligingly headed towards the entrance. Eliminating all four men was the only way she could escape without leaving a trail. She quickly took stock mentally of what resources she had to hand that might serve as weaponry: an aerosol pepper spray in her handbag and a designer umbrella. What she lacked in weapons she was going to have to make up for with a large dose of surprise and by finding her enemies' weaknesses. There was no doubt that all four men had been taking their own medicine during their delivery run, so that at least would slow down their reactions. Caroline launched into a pleading protest, begging the men not to hurt her, and offering to give them all her money and credit cards. She fumbled in her handbag as if looking for her purse, but took the opportunity to get the pepper spray ready for use as soon as they were out of range of the camera. Her pleas simply seemed to fuel their excitement. Ideally it would be best to take the officer and general first, in this case Ricky and Allan, but as they escorted her into the damp morning air, it was the other two thugs who were closest to her.

Caroline tightened her hold on the pepper spray and checked the nozzle was in position. Her spray was non-standard issue, with twice the strength of the stuff used on the streets, and guaranteed to immobilise and bring those bastards to their knees with one direct hit. This was going to be payback time for all those attacks they had got away with in the past: the hunter was quickly going to become the hunted. Still pleading plaintively, she discreetly took a few steps backwards as if cowering away from her attackers until she was at a good distance to take aim. With military precision, Caroline let them have it.

One jet blasted straight into Rick Smith's left eye, the second zapped Allan straight in the face. Quickly she gave a booster shot to each man to stop them advancing. Seeing what had happened, the third guy came bounding over but was stopped in his tracks by Allan Smith, who doubled over with his hands covering his face and stumbled backwards into his mate. The fourth guy steered clear of the collision and lunged towards Caroline. It was time to reach for her second weapon – the umbrella. As if wielding a sabre, she drew the umbrella up to head height and propelled it forward into the man's eye. The cry of pain echoed around the empty car park. Caroline quickly turned around to deal with the third guy who was now up on his feet again. She grabbed him by the hair and flung him sideways against a concrete waste bin whose unyielding sides instantly restructured the contours of his face.

Ricky was still fumbling around, clearly trying to make a retreat to the wagon. Caroline knew that he couldn't be allowed to get away and quickly assessed her best plan of attack. Luck was on her side. Ricky suddenly misjudged the kerb and fell over. She seized the advantage with a well-placed kick straight between his legs while he was still down. Reaching for her trusty pepper spray, she pulled him up by the lapels and released a direct jet of spray into his eyes. His cry of pain performed a duet with the shriek emitted by Allan, who, crawling across the grass verge, had not only put his hand into a loose dog turd but stupidly then rubbed his still stinging eye with the same hand. Caroline wondered whether he realised that the turd alone was a hundred times more dangerous than anything her pepper spray could inflict on him! "Serves him right for never clearing up after his own dogs," she told herself. They say there is nothing like a woman scorned and at that moment Francis was that woman!

The next afternoon, Francis relayed his story and the spot of trouble that he'd encountered. You could hear his proud satisfaction that he had finally been given the opportunity to be judge, jury and executioner and deliver the kind of punishment that those criminals had all too often dodged in the past. On behalf of Charlotte, I thanked him heartily and asked him to make sure that he passed on my gratitude to Caroline too!

Reg was less impressed. "So, you got yourself into a spot of bother, old boy?"

"Yes, you could say that," admitted Francis.

"Are you ok?"

"Yes, thanks."

"Are you sure?" Reg persisted.

"Yes honestly, but it was a bit of a close call. I'm pretty confident that nothing was caught on camera, and certainly no-one was hanging around outside in that miserable, freezing fog."

"Well, I can assure you that no 'wanted' notices have been issued for an attractive twenty-three-year old wearing stilettos and armed with an umbrella," joked Reg. "I should imagine the Smiths would be too bloody embarrassed to let anyone know what really happened on their Friday night out!"

Francis chuckled. "If anyone dared to ask they'd just say they had come across some rival gang members trying to elbow in on their patch," he agreed.

I found it difficult to be as relaxed about the ordeal as Reg and Francis clearly were. My problem was that I didn't have the training or experience of these two army boys. For them an encounter like last night's was a welcome chance to get some practice in. If there was a job to be done these men would be the first to volunteer and see it through from start to finish!

Francis felt there was nothing more to be gained from watching Stephan Smith from the usual hideout. If we needed more proof about Smith's habits and the Sunday morning paper run, then Francis needed to be at the parade of shops to establish the exact timing of Smith's routine. He suspected that after Friday night's escapade, Smith would be bound to take notice of any single woman within a two-mile radius, so he stuck to his rambler outfit, adding a beard and hanging a compass around his neck to complete the look. He parked a couple of roads away from the parade and spent the next half an hour browsing in the shop windows and reading the small ads. Almost to the minute that Francis had predicted, Stephan Smith rolled up in his car. A quick glance told Francis that Smith was on his own, apart from the security of his two Dobermans. Francis quickly went inside the shop, picked up a basket and positioned himself in an aisle that overlooked the checkout counter. He selected a packet of trifle mix and pretended to become engrossed in the ingredients panel. It was only a few seconds before Smith entered the shop and headed straight for the counter. Two young boys had bought a multitude of mixed sweets and the shopkeeper was trying to tally up the total. Smith reached over the boys' heads and handed the shopkeeper a clutch of lottery tickets to be checked. He then strolled across to the newspapers, picked out two copies each from three different shelves, and then went over to the chiller cabinet for a couple of cans of energy drink. He slapped his papers down on the counter and pulled open one of the cans to take a drink.

By this time a small queue had formed of about half a dozen people, but Francis could see that the shopkeeper had learned it was better to let Smith jump the queue and leave the shop as quickly as possible. It simply wasn't worth trying to reason with him, nor was he prepared to let his customers be intimidated by the man. Unfortunately, a gentleman in his late seventies was made of sterner stuff, and stepped forward to point out to Smith that others were waiting.

"Fuck off, you old git," snarled Smith.

The man reeled back in shock, and moved to the back of the queue where he was quietly comforted by neighbours. An uneasy silence followed while Smith ordered his weekly lottery tickets and paid for his goods. As soon as the foul-mouthed customer had left, the shopkeeper apologised wholeheartedly to his customers and explained why he had made it a policy to serve Smith first. As Francis listened to the angry comments of the other shoppers about Smith's outburst, he knew like his fellow HOLI members that the days of talking were over.

Francis stuck around a little longer, as he could see that the shopkeeper was now engaged in conversation with a sympathetic customer who wanted to know more about 'that foulmouthed berk'. Letting his tongue loosen, the shopkeeper revealed that Smith had been a regular for the last year or so. He came in every Sunday without fail to have his lottery tickets checked and to pick up the papers and a couple of cans of drink. "He always spends fifty pounds on new lottery tickets," he added. "Why would you bother when you've already got millions?"

The woman shook her head in bewilderment and left the shop tut-tutting at the morning's events.

There were three useful things that Francis learned from Smith's outburst. One was that having now seen Smith in the flesh and close up, he was confident that Otis would carry off the role of his double comfortably. Second, watching Smith's whole persona change when he lashed out confirmed to Francis that when the snatch took place, Smith was going to be a force to be reckoned with. And third, HOLI now had the information it needed to push the green light.

In his daily report to Reg, it was agreed that he should spend the last week gathering as much footage of Smith as possible so that Otis could start working on his character and voice. Their concern was that although Smith and Otis looked the same, when Otis smiled or looked at someone, they felt warm and safe. With Smith, the look was only ever cold and sinister. Otis would need to undergo a complete change of character to be convincing in his role.

Unshaven and bundled up in a parka that concealed two mobiles and a couple of spycams, Francis followed Smith on his two main outings of the week: to the cash and carry and to the dog races. He hovered in aisles behind a piled-high trolley, joined the same queue at the checkout and bustled around in the crowds at the greyhound stadium to capture as much as possible of Smith's mannerisms and language for Otis to study.

Before returning to Spain with the camper van, Francis tracked one more newspaper run just to make sure that absolutely nothing had changed. It was good news for HOLI: they were dealing with a creature of habit.

We met Francis at the bottom of 'safari pass', the nickname we'd given to the six-mile track leading to Reg's place. As we passed the Romma's farm we were greeted as always with smiles and waves. Now that I'd become such a regular visitor, I almost felt like I was one of the family. Even so, the increased visits and the sight of a motorhome must have made them curious. I pointed this out to Reg, who was ahead of the game as usual.

"You're right, Paul, but don't worry. I've got an idea what to do. Let's discuss it back at the house."

Shake and Spear were at the house to greet us, but we'd be

needing something fiercer to act as our security guards once we had Smith in captivity. Once inside, Reg made a large pot of tea as we settled down to discuss the next stage of our operation.

In a couple of weeks' time, Tottenham was due to play Barcelona FC in the Champions League. HOLI would travel back to England for the match – the perfect alibi given that three of us were Spurs supporters. That said, when Otis and I broke all ties with England and came over to Spain, we had effectively changed teams and started supporting Barcelona. We had only been to a handful of matches, but rarely missed a game on TV. Reg said that the two of us would stay as Barcelona supporters, leaving Francis and him to side with Tottenham. It turned out that Reg had been a Spurs fan since he was a boy, but Francis was a rugby man, and so would need a bit of coaching from Reg. With Spurs and Barcelona flags adorning the dashboard, mascots hanging from the mirrors and us wearing our supporter shirts, we would have the perfect cover to satisfy Alison, Customs and the police. One of our hot spots was being able to rely on the police and Customs believing that the sedated Stephan Smith in the back of our van was nothing more than a worse-for-wear supporter who had over-indulged his enthusiasm for his team.

"What odds would you give us for getting stopped at the border?" I asked cautiously.

"To be honest, Paul, I don't know. It would be best if Barcelona won, because if we were stopped and searched, the police would see a funny side to a pissed-up Spurs fan drowning his sorrows. Let's hope we just sail through."

It was agreed on arrival in England, that Francis would return to his campsite and that we three would check in to a local four-star hotel. Over the following two days we could get ourselves familiar with the area and the location of Smith's place, and, of course, go to the match. On the Saturday, Francis would pick up the van and equipment and then the snatch plan would come into play.

"Is everybody happy with the snatch plan that Francis has drawn up?" asked Reg. We had already seen a rough layout, but Francis had changed a couple of things since his last week of surveillance and wanted to run it past us for final approval. He cleared his throat before launching into a read-through.

"The plan is to snatch Smith on the Sunday morning. At eight-thirty, Reg, Otis and Paul will arrive at the campsite in my mini and leave it in the visitors' car park. Arrangements will already have been made to leave it there for a couple of weeks. After conferring about any last-minute changes, Reg and Otis will drive the Transit van to No. 5 lay-by – it's highlighted on here." Francis handed each of us a map for information.

"It's essential that you're in position by nine-thirty. Paul and I will take the camper van to High Green Lane and park up opposite the turning to Wardrobe Lane. We'll both have chains on board as well as notices advising drivers that the road is closed while tree-felling is in operation. You can see on the map where these will have to be positioned. They'll be easy to attach by chains and hooks so that they make a full-width barrier. I'm going to transform the camper van into an operating 'theatre' internally and horsebox externally. As you know there's an equestrian centre nearby, and while on surveillance I noticed that plenty of traffic for the centre goes down Wardrobe Lane instead of the easier route further along. This gave me an idea that'll give us more time for the snatch. If Stephan Smith is convinced that the vehicle blocking Wardrobe Lane is a horsebox it will buy us precious seconds. Any questions so far?" Francis paused, but we had nothing to say.

"Between nine forty-five and ten, Stephan Smith will pass you on his paper run. You will phone us straightaway, so that Paul and I can get down to the first entrance for Wardrobe Lane and position ourselves where the road is still wide enough for two vehicles to pass. You'll then let us know when Smith is on his return journey so that we can move further down the lane and wait in the designated spot. You will now be following Smith at a safe distance so that he suspects nothing. Once you get into Wardrobe Lane you get out and place your sign across the road. This must take no more than thirty seconds. When Smith reaches the back of the camper/horsebox he'll have to stop. I'll be kitted out as a horsewoman, not for pleasure but hopefully to buy us some more time." As I come round the side of the camper van I'll be holding a road atlas. This will be my shield for the dart gun that's going to knock him out. I'll be carrying a second gun for the two dogs. My plan is that once I'm close enough to the driver's door, I'll ram the shield at an angle to wedge open the window and prevent the dogs snapping at me. With the dart gun pointing at him, I'll instruct Smith to put the car in park and pull the handbrake on. By this time Paul should be positioned at the front of the car pointing an Oozie replica at Smith's head. Reg and Otis will be behind in the Transit van blocking him in. The hardest part will be to get darts into the dogs, which will probably be going ballistic by this stage. The tranquiliser will knock them out cold in about thirty to sixty seconds. Reg, you will have to carry some back-up guns as well. Otis, you will have the second Oozie replica.

"We then blindfold Smith and force him into the van. Once we have him inside and his blindfold is removed, he'll find himself laid out on a table in the plastic-lined 'operating theatre' with a television screen in front of him. There will be two restraining belts holding him down. Paul drives the camper, Otis takes Smith's car minus the dogs, and Reg follows behind in the Transit. Our destination is marked on the map. It's the waste ground with two old Dutch barns. We'll have to drive past Smith's mansion, but it's unlikely that anyone will be about."

"The plan's very good, Francis," said Otis, "but the only problem I can see is Smith's car window. What if he keeps it closed?"

"Good point," replied Francis. "On the three occasions that I've seen Smith on his paper run, the driver's window has been down regardless of the weather. I think he does it for the dogs because they've always got their muzzles sticking out. If, however, the window is closed on the day, I will have to use my womanly wiles to tease Smith's ego and sexual prowess to do the job for us!"

Francis was putting himself on the front line for this operation. Although I still couldn't get my head around his cross-dressing, it might be the difference between the success and failure of our mission.

Reg continued with the plan. "Once at the Dutch barns, we will strip Smith and put the D/D on him. The snuff movie will be playing on a constant loop on the television screen, and there will be a permanent caption carrying the reminder 'This is what will happen to you if you don't follow our orders'. Once the D/D is on, we will dress Smith and place the two hidden cameras on him. He will be fitted with an earphone and given a list of what needs to be brought from his home: passport, driving licence, birth certificate, all credit cards and some cash, plus a suitcase with clothes. These will be itemised, as he's unlikely to be thinking straight by this stage."

"He will then be told what our intentions are, what we want from him and what we want him to do. First he must drive home and get his stuff. If anyone asks what's going on, he is to tell them he has an important meeting in Amsterdam with some Russians. We will then tell him why we are kidnapping him. He will be told it's for a £5 million ransom. Given the man's wealth, I'm confident that he won't think twice about losing that sum in exchange for his freedom and will cooperate. He then needs to drive unaccompanied (and that means no dogs!) to the Channel Tunnel and buy a return ticket on his credit card. Once in France, he will need to get on the motorway for Dunkirk, pulling off at a large service area just before the turnoff for the town. In the overflow car park, two men will meet him and remove the D/D from him. Accompanied by the men, he will then drive to Amsterdam and check in at a hotel where a reservation has already been made for him. The next day, the escorts will take him to the bank to transfer the money to an offshore account.

What Smith doesn't know is that when the two men get into the car at Dunkirk they will be armed with tranquilisers. Once he is sedated, we will transfer him to the camper van, dress him in a Spurs kit and douse him in alcohol so he stinks like a brewery. Otis, now dressed in Smith's clothes and carrying

Smith's passport and belongings, will continue on to Amsterdam and stay at the hotel, while we drive through the night, hopefully reaching home at about eight the next morning. We will then transfer Smith to his new abode for the next two weeks."

CHAPTER EIGHT

"THE FIRST THING THAT STEPHAN SMITH WILL SEE when he wakes up in his cell will be this, gentlemen." Reg held up for display two large books. They were not very thick, possibly about a dozen pages each, covered and bound with a plastic cover.

"This one is for us and this one is for Mr Smith. Both will be destroyed once HOLI's mission is completed." He passed the books round the table for us to take a closer look. On seeing the words written on the front cover, a sick feeling deep in my stomach erupted.

STEPHAN SMITH
SENTENCE OF DEATH
BORN 21 JUNE 1969
EXECUTED 29 FEBRUARY 2008

"What I've done here is self-explanatory and simple enough that even Smith can follow it. More tea, anyone?" he asked, ever the thoughtful host.

Clearly the plan had left our throats dry and we answered, "Yes, please," in unison. Reg duly went off to the kitchen leaving the three of us to look over the books. The first page read:

Stephan Smith, you are under a death sentence to be carried out in two hours' time within the confines of this cell. Death will be by drowning. Your cell will fill with ice-cold water. If you're lucky you'll die from the cold before the water fills the entire space. Your lifeless body will then be filled with alcohol and drugs and dumped in a canal in Amsterdam. The police will be left with no alternative but to return a verdict of accidental death at your inquest. But that's not all. Your death will become the trigger for a string of carefully timed deaths to befall selected members of your family, starting with the lovely Tanya Smith, your mother. We'll remember to include your brothers, Rick and Sam — perhaps a car crash or cocaine overdose would be suit them best — and extend our services to your trusted friend and conniving solicitor, David Buxton. Overdoses, freak accidents, unfortunate ends – be in no doubt, these things WILL happen.

If revenge is the way to resolve crime, then Reg had found solutions that even the most hardened terrorist might have thought twice about. He knew that Stephan Smith would quickly see that he was in a no-win situation. Nothing would compensate for what Smith had done to my daughter but seeing that monster's face would be another a welcome taster of justice. For a moment I pictured myself in Smith's situation. Pure fear, and the most extreme variety at that, would run through his mind. To put it bluntly, if I had just been on the receiving end of the same physical experience and ultimatum that had been delivered to Smith over the past twenty-four hours I would be literally shitting myself — which was exactly what Reg had intended. At the bottom of the page was the word 'REPRIEVE' in large capital letters followed by 'PTO'. I turned over and the letter continued:

The execution of your and your family will be halted only if we receive your full cooperation. You have two hours from the time shown on the clock on the wall. You will answer each of these questions fully and accurately. Any attempt to conceal the truth will result in death. Any unanswered questions will result in death. The lives of you and your family depend on you telling the truth, for the first time in your life.

1. *How many people have you, your family or associates killed? Give details.*
2. *Name your suppliers.*
3. *How do your drugs get into the country?*
4. *Name your main dealers and how you supply them.*
5. *Name each of your UK and offshore accounts.*

Remember, only the truth will save your life.

I looked up from the book to gauge the others' reactions. Was Smith really going to play along with this?

"Do you think he'll buy it, Reg?" Otis asked the question that was on all our lips.

"Put it this way," said Reg, "what would you do in the same situation? At the end of the day, the only thing he cares about is his money and himself. He's got enough money to pay off the ransom, and he's got the answers that'll buy him his freedom. Getting the answers to those five questions will be the difference between success and failure. By noon on that day, we'll know for sure; after that it will be down to Malt, our fifth member."

"Who?"

Reg owed us an explanation. "You don't need to know how Malt and I came into contact, what you do need to appreciate is that his involvement is crucial in closing this operation for us.

Along with a love of good whisky – hence the nickname! – Malt has an unblemished career of near on forty years in the police force. When retirement day finally came, he vowed to continue his pursuit of those criminals who still needed to be brought to account for their endless crimes. When Malt reads the contents of the recorded delivery letter that we send him, it will offer him the crowning moment to his lifelong commitment to justice. Our letter will give him enough information and evidence for him to know he has a watertight case against the Smiths. This is why the answers to those five questions we put to Smith are going to be so important. Armed with this information, Malt will use all his years of experience to get his superiors to make a fourth and successful raid on Smith's mansion and uncover the full extent of that family's dirty dealings."

"Sounds like we've got the equivalent of our fifth Beatle," I joked, "and I'm liking the sound of him already!"

"So let me take up where I left off, gents," said Reg, swiftly moving on with rest of the plan. "Otis, using Smith's credit card, will open accounts in Amsterdam, Switzerland and Andorra and then return back to Amsterdam four days later where he will meet up with Francis. Using Smith's mobile, we'll text instructions to his brothers to arrange storage facilities at various locations for a big haul that's due in. They'll no doubt phone back to double-check his instructions and that'll be when Otis transforms into Smith. He'll tell them that he's had information that the price of cocaine is set to quadruple in the next three weeks so they're to buy up as much as possible and place it in storage."

"Why so much cocaine?" asked Francis.

"Because when the police carry out their raid on the day that we tell them to, they will have no trouble in finding a quantity of cocaine with a street value of millions which the Smiths have been told to keep back for collection by Stephan's new business associates." Reg paused for a second.

"However, a more immediate and major problem facing us is Smith's prison – the cargo container." He passed around a sheet of sketches that showed the interior and exterior of the cell. "We need to get the container buried underground before the start of the wild boar season in a few weeks' time. It's the only time of year that you'll get visitors up here, usually accompanied by the Romma's who always make a point of calling in to recount the day's hunting and share a glass or two of wine. If we're going to look like a professional operation, this cell has got to convince Smith that he's dealing with the real thing, not amateurs who have waded in right out of their depth. The fittings have got to be state-of-the-art – all stainless steel and hi-tech – you know the kind I thing I mean."

"The same goes for the snuff movie, but we can sort that out next month. I am in the process of buying some equipment and special effects which should help."

Making the snuff movie was something I was dreading, so to take my mind off it, I started to study the sketches in more detail. They looked pretty impressive. Good job I had the DIY skills and experience to take on the challenge. At least it would be an opportunity for me to shine at my specialist subject too, just like Francis and Reg with their military know-how. All the same, even with four pairs of hands, it was going to take a fair bit of time and effort to get the cell looking exactly like Reg's vision on paper.

"And now for the bad news," announced Reg. "Christmas is cancelled!" Catching sight of my jaw heading south, he explained. "I know it's the traditional 'family' time, Paul, but it also provides us with the perfect cover for sinking the container. If the four of us started work on the day before Christmas Eve and carried on right through until the next morning, it would give us fifteen hours in which to dig the hole, place the container inside, get rid of the waste soil and make good so it looks as if nothing has happened."

"A good man on a JCB and one in a tip truck could do that job in three to four hours," said Otis.

"That's the problem, Otis. We can't use a JCB or any other large plant equipment." He explained about the problem with the over-helpful Romma's. "No, the best we can do is hire a mini kabuta. One of those will fit in Paul's trailer and we can throw a tarpaulin over it so he can drive past the Romma's place without it being noticed. Together with the two Land Rovers, a couple of winches, spades and forks plus my trusty old Ebro, I think we can complete the job in one night. A bottle of double malt whisky says we can do it." Reg's wager sealed the deal.

"You forgot one thing we need though," I pointed out.

"What's that, Paul?" asked Reg.

"A bloody miracle!" I replied.

Before leaving, I suddenly remembered that Alison had asked me to invite Francis and Reg to spend Christmas Day with us. The locals tended to wait for *Los tres reyes magos* at the beginning of January for their celebrations, which was a festival that we always joined in, but we couldn't bear to let the twenty-fifth of December pass without Christmas dinner, trimmings and presents. To my surprise, I found that Charlotte had already invited Francis, while Reg had already accepted an invitation from the Romma's to join them for dinner that day.

And so it was that on the twenty-third, while others were busying themselves for Christmas festivities, wrapping presents, decorating the tree, icing the cake or welcoming loved ones and friends, the four of us set about digging the biggest hole of our lives. I had brought the digger and a dumper, plus four jerry cans of diesel which I could easily see us getting through. There was no time for a practice run or going offsite to get supplies; this had got to be the real thing.

As day broke, our task was near completion. While I washed down the dumper and digger which had served us well throughout the night, Francis and Otis finished camouflaging the top of the container with straw, dirt and dust. Where the cargo container had stood for years was now covered in bushes, saplings and weeds. With the job done, we each took a welcome hot shower, and sat down to demolish a breakfast of eggs, bacon and hot coffee. Slowly we started to feel human again. Even the ex-army boys admitted that they'd hit the wall during the early hours of the morning and couldn't remember the last time they'd taken on a physical challenge on that scale. I felt quite proud of myself that I had kept up with them from start to finish.

After dropping off the digger and dumper I returned home hoping to catch up on some much-needed sleep. Unfortunately Alison had other ideas. Charlotte had gone to do some last-minute shopping, when really she should have been helping out at home, so I found myself roped into galley duties for a couple of hours before managing to snatch a four-hour kip on the settee. That evening we joined in the village get-together for Christmas Eve. There was a tempting smell of burning pine coming from one of the restaurants, and the happy sound of chatter in the air. Alison and I joined in, greeting our neighbours and catching up on their news. While chatting to a fellow builder, I caught sight of Charlotte and Francis sitting on the side of the fountain in the plaza, holding hands. When I looked back for a second time, to make sure my eyes weren't fooling me, Charlotte and Francis were in the processing of taking it in turns to peck each other on the cheek. Without appearing abrupt, I excused myself from further conversation and found myself a quiet corner of the square where I could contemplate.

For a father to think about his daughter's sex life is difficult, but three years ago I was forced to confront it. After Charlotte was raped, we were advised that it would be very difficult for her to form relationships again; it would take a very special person to be allowed to get close to her. Thankfully Charlotte had, in time, formed a circle of lovely friends, both boys and girls, but nothing more intimate than 'just friends'. From what I had just seen, I was beginning to wonder whether Francis might be that special person. Time would tell, I imagined.

Christmas Day started with the opening of presents. This was traditionally something I always left to Alison to sort out, but on this occasion she had found it difficult to choose presents for Reg and Francis. Fortunately I had an idea that would satisfy both men's passion for a spot of adventure – a ride in a hot-air balloon. I remembered that Francis had once mentioned that it was one of those things he'd always wanted to try, and for Reg, well it would make a change from travelling in the cockpit!

From the screams of Alison and Charlotte, I knew that Francis had bought them the perfect gift – designer shoes from Jimmy Choo. Who else but Francis would know his way around women's fashion so well?

After a traditional dinner with all the trimmings, Otis got ready for a party he'd been invited to back in Barcelona. He tentatively asked Francis and Charlotte whether they would like to come and they both eagerly accepted his offer. Charlotte actually wanting to go to a party? Things were changing!

By nine o'clock Alison announced she was absolutely knackered and headed off to bed, leaving me alone with a bottle of very expensive brandy – my present from Reg, who else? A campfire is often described as an outdoor TV; I was finding our open fire in the lounge just as mesmerising. As I watched the flames perform their dance routine, I reflected on how lucky I was to have such a loving family and good friends. It had been a special Christmas. Only the thought of what lay ahead dampened my spirits, so I offered up a quick prayer that what we were doing would succeed and that everyone who was precious to me would not suffer if we failed.

* * *

Now that we had stepped into the New Year, we had just over five weeks to complete our preparations. Francis and Otis were working hard on making Otis look, talk and act like Smith. In between their rehearsals, Francis needed to make three return trips to England. One to check that Smith was sticking to his same routine, second to buy the guns, and third to sort out the Transit van and equipment for the roadblocks. Reg and I spent most of our afternoons underground, fitting out the cell until it looked the part. The month simply flew past.

There was a scary start to February when two male wild boars managed to get into the courtyard, where Reg and I were engrossed in a discussion about the new library. Both beasts stood and looked at us for a second until Spear and Shake came storming out to our rescue and gave the boars no choice but to beat a hasty retreat. Within a couple of minutes the Romma's had arrived with a few friends, all carrying guns and ready to kill. There was much disappointment when we explained that the visitors had exited stage left, so Reg often them a couple of bottles of wine and some tapas as consolation prizes. We were all about to walk into the house when old man Romma remarked, "One's gone." Reg and I froze as we saw the old man looking in the direction of the five remaining containers. "There used to be six."

He was a grand old man of eighty-seven, who still went out hunting with the boys; it was only his bandy old legs which couldn't stop a pig in a passage that let him down on occasions. My mind went into overdrive trying to find a convincing lie to offer him. How come we hadn't prepared some suitable stories for just such an event as this? So much for the best-laid plans. As it happened, Manuel, the eldest son, saved the day.

"Dad, you always reckon you see six when you cheat at dominoes! We'd put you in a home if only they would have you." This got a big laugh; it was an ongoing joke with the Romma's. The old boy took one last glance at the containers, shook his head and went inside for some food.

The snuff movie was the last job to be completed before we left for England. I was a bit of an innocent in that I'd no idea that such things existed. Francis, our man of a thousand experiences, had filled me in about the perverse pleasure that some people found in watching humans and animals being tortured and killed. It made me feel physically sick. Reg was confident that Smith would probably have a couple of these films in his DVD collection at home. He was exactly the type of character that took pleasure from watching violence and suffering. Our movies were going to be just two minutes in length. Francis and I would play the victims, Reg would direct the choreography and operate the cameras and Otis would play the guard. He needed to keep his face out of shot, so his back would be to the camera for most of the time.

The last time I had 'acted' was at the tender age of four, playing a shepherd in the school nativity. I don't remember much, but my mum said that I completely forgot my lines, and I've never been back on stage since. I'm always happy to 'have a go', but my real reluctance was having to get naked, and in front of my friends to boot! In adulthood, Alison was the only person to have seen me starkers, and I would have preferred to keep it that way. Of course, stripping off was second nature for the army boys. Even though there wasn't much chance of getting any sympathy from them, I reasoned that honesty was an integral part of operation HOLI, so it was my duty to tell them that I wasn't keen on getting naked.

The weather had been near freezing for the past week and today brought a layer of white frost across the ground. The sun would make an appearance later, but for now the sky was grey. Local winegrowers were starting to worry that the prolonged cold would affect their vines. It was the main topic of conversation in every bar that week. For HOLI, though, we had more pressing matters to discuss as we were heading for England in just two weeks' time. As we sat round the table discussing our parts in the movie, I plucked up the courage to tell them that I wasn't happy about being naked. There was a polite silence. Always the one to take the lead, Reg leapt to his feet and barked out his orders. "Stand up, all of you. Strip down to your socks and shoes, we're going to run to the first dry river and back. The last one makes lunch."

We all did as we were told and removed our layers right down to our birthday suits. Now I'm a pretty poor cook, but I'm even less of a sprinter. We shuffled out of the house and as soon as we left the confines of the yard, Otis and Francis broke out in front, leaving me to focus on their two white arses disappearing into the distance. Reg and I were doing about half their speed, so it wasn't long before we met them coming back, with Francis in the lead.

"All we need now is for one of the Romma's to stroll into our path," I muttered. "Try explaining this little escapade!" I kept up a decent pace, surprising myself that I'd made it this far. On the return leg, I forced myself into a sprint, but Reg was having none of it and we crossed the line neck and neck, laughing our heads off. Reg's idea had worked a treat.

The leftover rolls of plastic that we used to line the motorhome came in useful as backdrops for the film shoot. We chose to film in the library since it was the largest room and the easiest place to close off from unexpected visitors. Reg set the scene for us.

"The condemned men, you two, will be brought in to this white-lined room. You'll both be wearing white disposable boiler suits, which you will be asked in Russian to remove. You will be given a pair of these crotchless boxer shorts to put on." He held up a pair of black boxers that had a large hole in the back and front.

On closer inspection I could feel and see the outline of small black plastic pipes that had been sewn in. All the pipes were cut at a right angle giving what ever came out a larger spray.

"Probably the best thing to do is give you a live demonstration." Reg looked across at Francis. "Let's go for it."

Francis stripped off and put the boxers on. Eight pipes had fitted connections that came out of the back of the boxers. Another eight pipes came out from under the polythene floor. Reg connected them together, and then went over to the table in the centre of the room to make some checks on a large laptop device which had loads of wires coming out of it.

"You had better stand back," warned Reg. "Ready Francis?"

"Yep."

"One, two, three."

"Fucking hell!"

There was an almighty bang and a red and white flash all around Francis. A thick layer of smoke enveloped his torso and suddenly something splattered onto my face. I instinctively wiped it and found blood on my hands. "Shit, he's bleeding," I gasped.

"Keep calm, Paul, he's fine," assured Reg with a grin on his face.

Francis started screaming something in Russian and fell to

the floor. Reg paused the cameras.

He picked up a pan from his equipment shelf, while Francis removed his boxers and spread his legs wide apart. The contents of the pan – four chicken innards that had been boiled in water to make them look scorched – were carefully placed between Francis's legs. From a plastic bucket, Reg pulled out a large thin piece of cow's liver and laid it over the genitals. Next he added fragments of charred boxer shorts to the thighs, legs and stomach and, for a finishing touch, used a spray gun of fake blood to make Francis look suitably splattered. Returning to the table, Reg switched on the camera and cued Francis to start his Oscar-winning performance of a dying prisoner, writhing on the floor like a man who had just had his genitals blown off. It was sick, disgusting and bloody convincing. In a grand finale, Reg went up to Francis with a gun and shot him twice in the head. Two red dots appeared on his forehead. We looked on in stunned silence until the dead man promptly sat up and declared, "Your turn, Paul."

Reg had left absolutely nothing to chance in making the film. Special effects, stage make-up, even two Russian army uniforms for him and Otis to wear. This film needed to reduce Smith to a quivering wreck. It took six hours and endless takes before Reg was satisfied that he had enough material to work with. Two days later, with the help of an editing suite, he proudly gave us a private viewing of his creations. Unshaven and pallid looking, Francis and I made a convincing pair of condemned men. Alison had complained that my recent haircut had been two short and made me look like a criminal. She was right, my spiky short hair was the finishing touch to my desperate appearance. Of course,

I'll never be able to look at chicken in the same way from this day onwards.

* * *

It was the twentieth of February and the big day had arrived. We set off just before six in the morning. Reg drove down the track ahead of us to leave his Land Rover at the restaurant. There was a good chance we might need it to pull the camper when we returned, as the track had taken a battering over the winter and we couldn't afford to get stuck.

When we reached the border, it was the busiest time of day and Spanish Customs were content to wave us through. The French side merely stopped us to look at our passports. As we drove away from the passport control office, Reg voiced our thoughts, "Let's hope it goes that easily for us on the way back."

CHAPTER NINE

IF DECEPTION WAS THE ORDER OF THE DAY, then my three partners in crime were giving a first-class performance. We had caught the first ferry out of Calais heading for Dover. Reg had bought a couple of newspapers and Francis a glossy magazine. We made our way to the large lounge bar at the stern of the boat. Reg found a couple of 'friends' in the form of a pint of Guinness and the ear of an attractive bar stewardess, while Francis kicked off his shoes and made himself comfortable on one of the sofas. Using the arm of the sofa as a pillow, he immersed himself in his glossy, reaching out a hand occasionally for a Danish pastry and large cappuccino. Otis had also opted for a continental breakfast. He then found himself a comfy armchair and was engrossed in a novel that he had borrowed from Reg's library.

I marvelled how the three of them were the epitome of coolness. It was the exact opposite of how I was feeling right now. From the moment we had driven onto the ship, I had begun to feel sick and confused. This was nothing to do with seasickness; the Channel was flat calm this morning. What I was experiencing was an in-your-face visit from reality and it had given me a mighty large smack in the mouth. It must be how a prisoner felt on being moved to the solitary confinement of a condemned cell when the inevitable was about to happen. We were soon to kidnap an out-and-out gangster and relieve him of his millions. This was the stuff of movies, but our little plot was about to happen without a film crew or director – this one was for real.

Seeing the three of them looking so calm simply made me feel worse. I would never admit it to them, but I was jealous at the way they were taking it all in their stride. I made my excuses about being the worst sailor ever and needing some fresh air, and headed up to the deck, leaving behind a fresh pot of tea that I simply couldn't face. Up at the stern of the ship I sat down on one of the many benches; there was no one else around. We were now out in the English Channel. The salt breeze and sound of seagulls took me back to childhood holidays and I let myself enjoy memories of a less-complicated life. I don't know how long I sat there, just staring down at the decking trying to come to terms with what we were about to do. How could I pull out now? For one thing it would haunt me for the rest of my life, constantly asking myself why I didn't do it. And then there were Reg, Francis and Otis. How could I tell them I was out, purely because your dad, your friend is a coward, who at this moment is scared of his own shadow? No, I was in too deep now. Turning the clock back was not an option.

"You alright, Dad?" I had closed my eyes for a few seconds to shut out the world. At the sound of my son's voice, I looked up to see that Otis, along with Reg and Francis, had come to check on me. They had known something was wrong.

"We sensed you're anxious about something, probably Sunday." Reg had hit the nail on the head.

Being upfront with the rest of the team was the only way to get through this dilemma. "I don't think I'm up to it. You three seem to be able to contemplate the whole operation, the kidnapping and possibly murder, like it was nothing. Ever since we embarked on this plan of snatching Smith I've been unable to sleep, eat or even have a proper dump." I composed myself for a second. "I'm shit scared."

"Scared? You're the bravest of the four of us, you damn fool," Reg came straight back at me.

"How do you work that out?" I asked.

"Simply because we are the professionals, we've been trained. That's not to say we're not scared; a man who says that he has no fear is a bloody liar. We are a four-man team about to embark on a four-man job. If you want out, then operation HOLI is cancelled. We wouldn't think any less of you. If you don't think you can handle it, say now."

"Sorry." Reg's stern words snapped me out of it. I looked at all three of them and promised, "I'll be okay."

"We know you will, old boy," said Reg with a reassuring pat on my shoulder.

"There's something way more important that you need to face today, Paul," said Francis. "Alison and Charlotte gave me strict instructions to make sure you part with some money at the duty-free perfumery. I know just the person to point you in the right direction." Finishing his sentence with a very camp pose, Francis instantly restored us all to good spirits. Grabbing my arm, he steered me off to the shop, while Reg and Otis returned to the comfort of the lounge bar.

As I would be the driver on the day of the snatch, the drive to Henley was a good opportunity to familiarise myself with the camper van and with driving on the left again. Three years of living in Spain had eroded the memory of how much I hated driving in England. What should have been a two-hour journey took just over seven hours. It was three in the afternoon when we arrived at the campsite. Thanks to torrential rain and two accidents on the M25 car park, we crawled along the motorway at a snail's pace. The four of us passed the time, discussing and debating the fate of the country and what needed to be done to drag it out of the doldrums and take pride in itself once more.

Reg summed up our feelings pretty well. "I love Spain, I love England and, more importantly, I love my planet. That's why I've said, and I will say it again, that legalising certain drugs around the world and taxing them would see a sixty per cent growth in the economy. Overnight, there will be a significant fall in crime and drugs-related conflicts. Governments would be in control of the exports, not cartels."

Already well aware of the others' views on legalising drugs, I wasn't about to get in an argument on the subject. If three intelligent professionals believed that something needed to change, though, perhaps I did need to start listening. However, stubbornness upheld my own personal view that a completely drug-free society was the only solution.

At the campsite, Francis had already made arrangements with the site owners about where we would park up. He had struck a deal with them, explaining that he was in the process of moving to Spain to live and needed to be able to park his vehicles there for a few months. The site was virtually empty apart from half a dozen caravans, so space wasn't an issue and the upfront payment in cash smoothed the deal. Reg, Otis and I headed off to the nearby hotel, having arranged to meet up with Francis there later that evening. I felt a bit guilty staying in the comfort of a hotel while Francis slept in the camper, but it was done out of convenience for him as he needed space and privacy to transform from him to her on Sunday.

The hotel had quite a reputation for its excellent cuisine, but I wasn't able to appreciate the meal as much as I would have liked because of what lay ahead. Again, I looked on in envy at my partners' ability to switch off and enjoy the food and comfort of the hotel.

* * *

I realised as soon as I could smell the aroma of cooked onions and hamburgers drifting around White Hart Lane that I had made a mistake in turning my back on Tottenham to begin following a different team. Otis and I had been staunch Spurs supporters, as had been my father and my grandfather. It was simply because of what had happened to my family that I had focused the blame on England and anything connected with it. In short, I had cut off my nose to spite my face. Wiser now, I realised that it was the people who destroyed those places that I really wanted to eliminate from my life. Walking along to the stadium, I reminisced with Reg about matches won and lost, pubs, pie and mash shops and greasy spoon cafes which had all but disappeared. As soon as we stepped inside the ground, my betrayal was forgiven. Wrongs were about to be put right as Otis and I committed ourselves to Spurs once more. However, voicing our support today while standing knee-deep among Barcelona fans was probably not advisable.

To get to the quarter-final rounds of the Champions League

had been no small feat for the team. After the match, that was the only comforting thought I could hold on to as Spurs had managed to get more bookings than Westlife and more injuries than A & E on a Saturday night, topped off with a four-nil defeat. Otis and I had picked the wrong match for changing sides. From the sound of the ecstatic Barcelona fans, the second leg in their home city in two weeks' time was a foregone conclusion.

After picking up some souvenirs and silverware from the club shop, we took a taxi back to Henley. We had a few drinks in the hotel, three of us to drown our sorrows, before Francis headed off for the campsite and we went up to our rooms. The one good thing to have come out of the day was watching my old team play. It had provided a welcome chance to escape, if only for a couple of hours, from what lay ahead.

We now had a couple of days to kill before the main event on Sunday. Otis was driving with Francis over to Norfolk to stay with his parents. I had been invited but made my excuses for another time. Reg had arranged to meet up with old friends and had also invited me along. He tried his best to persuade me, joking that he'd need someone to carry him home, but I stuck to my excuses as I really didn't think I'd be good company with total strangers.

Left alone in the hotel, I found myself a quiet corner in the large conservatory that overlooked the river. A waiter brought me a pot of coffee and I sat back and just let the day unfold for a while. The tranquil scene looked inviting, so a little later I made the effort and took a walk along the Thames. The heavy frost from the previous night was still crisp on the ground and was clinging defiantly to the trees and hedgerows as the sun tried to loosen its hold on the day. Odd patches of crocus and early daffodils were pushing their way through the hard soil, and I wondered whether spring was dictating to winter or the other way round.

The sound of a cox's voice broke the silence as a team of six men came into view on the water. I watched their boat disappear from view, leaving only the sound of wild birds preparing for spring after surviving another hard winter. I reflected on the unusual chain of events that had brought me to this towpath today and Reg's conviction that operation HOLI was meant to be. As he had said many times, "If we don't do it, Paul, who will?" It was true, we were the last line of defence, the last chance to bring Stephan Smith and his family to justice. The British judicial system and the police had failed. Only the intervention of and change in government policy on some B- and C-class drugs would stop the escalation in the profiteering and violence that accompanied this trade. By the time I reached the market town of Marlow, I was feeling refreshed. The walk had certainly blown the cobwebs away. After a couple of pints I returned to my hotel, this time by taxi.

The next day Reg and I met at breakfast and discussed what we could do to kill time. Everything on our checklist had been completed. All we could do was wait, which is often the hardest job of all. We moved into the conservatory for coffee and read the papers for about an hour, after which we decided to take a walk in the opposite direction that I had taken the previous day. Clouds of vapour billowed from every breath we spoke. You could almost taste the coldness of the day in your lungs, it certainly was another cobweb-clearing day. We passed a marina and then found ourselves in a park that ran alongside the river. A mother and two young children were throwing bread for a group of swans grazing on the banks. We admired the simple pleasure on the faces of the children, but I could tell that Reg was tinged with sadness. The scene was bringing back memories of Elizabeth, the daughter he had effectively lost.

"You ok, Reg?" I asked cautiously.

"Yes, thanks. Just reminiscing. I used to take Elizabeth to Hyde Park to feed the ducks. She loved being taken to London Zoo for the pets' corner too." Reg smiled in an attempt to put a brave face on his pain.

I figured we were good enough friends now for me to ask a sensitive question. "Have you ever thought about trying to find her?"

"I think about it every day, Paul" came the reply.

I felt I had said the wrong thing, but Reg reassured me that it wasn't a problem. He explained that it was probably down to his stubbornness that he and Elizabeth, assuming she was still alive, had been kept apart. Her love and respect for her family had been stolen by drugs and their dealers, and few families had won that battle in trying to get their child back. The result every time was drug dealer – one, drug taker – nil.

Francis and Otis returned on Saturday, refreshed from their excursion to Norfolk. We met at the camp for a final run-through of the following day's schedule. Reg insisted on going through all one hundred and eighty-eight items on our checklist, which included everything from wet wipes to a spare tyre. Nothing was left to chance. The final point for discussion was the execution of Stephan Smith and the handgun. Francis had already checked and fired the weapon with the silencer on, but there was a golden rule among soldiers, each man checks his own weapon. I watched as Reg checked the handgun and loaded the bullets with ease and precision. He was a true professional in the way he handled the piece. Less impressive for me was the thought that the next time Reg touched the gun would be when I handed it to him to kill Smith.

With nothing more to discuss, we disbanded for a couple of hours before meeting up for a meal that evening in the hotel. Apart from two other tables the restaurant was empty. Our waiter, Henry, turned out to be a Tottenham boy too, and stood to chat with us for a while. He confided that this end of the market was feeling the recession, hence the lack of customers on a Saturday night. As usual, the rest of the team ate, drank and chatted with ease as though the next day wasn't important. As much as I tried to disguise my fear, my starter and main course told a different story.

When coffees and four large brandies arrived, Otis raised his glass. "I think the toast tonight gentlemen should be...." He didn't need to say any more. Our four glasses met in the centre of the table and in hushed voices we chimed, "To HOLI." The moment was poignant.

* * *

Sunday morning arrived. Down at the campsite, we transferred our cases into the Transit, parked up the mini and made our way to the camper, where we were met by an attractive young lady, Francis.

"Well, if Smith doesn't ask you out, I will," said Reg, trying to keep it light as always.

Just after nine-thirty we drove to our positions. We were some thirty yards from the entrance to Wardrobe Lane in a safe passing place. I got out and went to the kitbox to carry out my own transformation into a tree feller. We had jackets, hard hats, ear defenders and lumberjack shirts to make us look the part. To keep myself occupied, I then ran a quick double-check through the rest of the equipment, even though I knew full well that everything we needed was in place. Armed with traffic cones, hazard tape and the diversion sign, I prepared the cordon on the south entrance to Wardrobe Lane so that we could set it up in the tight turnaround time once Smith was in the lane. I attached one end of the tape as close to the hedge as possible, in the hope of deterring any walkers from entering.

Back in the van, I found Francis checking his make-up in the rear-view mirror. It was exactly what Charlotte and Alison did when they were in the car. He pouted his lips. "You don't think this looks too brassy, Paul?"

I shook my head. "You've got time to worry about lipstick when you're about to carry out a ruthless kidnap?"

"Well, a lady must look her best at all times," came the reply.

I took a look in the back of the van to check out the 'operating theatre'. The whole thing looked very clinical and sinister with its bizarre combination of leather straps, paper towels and plastic sheeting. I noticed that Francis had added a false number plate, HOR 5, to the disguise. Once we were in Wardrobe Lane, the awning would be pulled down to transform the van into a horsebox. Francis and I didn't speak. We exchanged half-hearted smiles and waited for the phone to ring. My mouth was dry again, so I reached for the bottle of water in my door pocket. At exactly that moment the mobile went off. Francis switched it onto loudspeaker. "Smith's car is in sight." There was a pause, then, "Fuck, there's a third dog and it's a Dogo."

Francis made a snap decision. "Paul will have to help me dart the dogs. I can't handle three by myself."

"So we're still good to go?" asked Reg.

"Good to go," confirmed Francis.

Still looking like something from the pages of OK magazine, Francis gave the order to move out. As we drove to the north end of Wardrobe Lane he outlined his plan for dealing with the third dog. He explained that the two Dobermans would defend their space with all their strength, but the Dogo – a fierce breed of dog from Argentina – would attack. In their homeland, they were capable of bringing down a cougar or wild boar and killing it.

"Letting Smith loose with an animal like that is crazy, let alone dangerous. And where did he get it from? They're banned in this country, not that breaking the law would bother him! It's going to take all my strength to stop that animal trying to get out of the window. I'll need both hands to use the shield to hold him back. You will need to dart the dogo as quickly as possible. Make sure you dart him twice. If the Dogo gets out we're in real trouble. There's my long leather coat in the back of the van. Once the dog's darted, you're going to wrap the coat over its head. I reckon it'll take a good thirty seconds before the Dogo stops fighting. Have you got that?" Francis was giving his orders in full military style.

I nodded. There were no words to express what I really felt.

We turned into the north end of Wardrobe Lane and parked up a few yards from the entrance where it was possible for two vehicles to pass. I got out and pulled down the awning and fixed the straw netting to either side of the van. Stepping back to examine my work, I was certain that nobody approaching from behind would question that they were stuck behind a horsebox. When I returned to the driver's seat I found Francis cannibalising his spare handbag into a second holster to carry the extra darts and guns needed.

"Try this." I fitted the belt in place, and put the darts and guns in the holster while Francis hung the leather coat over my head so it looked like a hooded cape. "There we go," he said. "Now you look like a cross between Dick Turpin and Billy the Kid!"

I was finding it hard to share the joke right now.

We returned to the waiting game. Once Smith had passed Reg and Otis in the lay-by we had only just over three minutes to drive down to our position and get ready to exit from the side door of the van. My guts were now doing somersaults inside me. If there were doubts in my mind about my importance in the team they were now dispelled. I was contributing to the most dangerous part of the plan so far and did not intend to let my team down. At least the weather was on our side. Misty with heavy drizzle, it would help to muzzle the sounds of the dogs and loud voices. The phone didn't get to the second ring. Francis had already responded. He put the phone back down on the dashboard and nodded at me to go. I started up the engine and moved down to the designated spot in Wardrobe Lane. The drizzle had now turned to heavy rain, which was all to our advantage.

"You ok, mate?" Francis asked. "Don't worry about anything else other than getting those two darts in that Dogo, Paul."

At that moment, Smith's car came into sight, slowly driving towards us in the rain. The sight of that car suddenly brought a flashback to the day of my mother's funeral. I had volunteered to wait outside for the hearse and its entourage to arrive. From the moment I saw my mother's coffin, I felt like I was watching the whole proceedings through someone else's eyes. My only explanation was that then, as now, it was my way of coping with not wanting to be there.

"Time for justice to be done, Paul." Francis snapped me out of my hiding place. "Remember what this man did to our Charlotte." The words 'our Charlotte' didn't fully register with me until much later that day. Smith's car had pulled to a halt a short distance behind our 'horsebox'. Francis got out and walked up to the tinted glass window of the driver's seat. "Good morning. Sorry to be a pain, but I'm lost. I don't suppose you could help me," he gushed huskily at Smith.

Hearing my cue, I leapt out ready to plant the first dart in the Dogo. Unfortunately, the leather coat got caught on the door handle in my haste to get out and the door swung me round almost removing my head from my shoulders. I quickly regained my balance and saw that, as Francis had predicted, the Dogo had gone for the attack. Half of its body was already outside the driver's window. Francis was using all his strength with the shield to hold him back. Its teeth had already reached the right arm of his jacket but luckily had only torn fabric not flesh. There was no shortage of body mass to aim for. My first dart hit the left side of his body, followed swiftly by the second. For the next 30 seconds I acted like a man possessed. I punched the dog straight in the face to stun it, then threw the coat over its head. I grabbed the animal in a half-nelson and pulled it from the car. Once the Dogo was on the ground I pinned its head to the floor with a hand press, while the rest of my body lay across its now twitching torso. The dog's growling was the last thing to subside.

"Its ok, Dad, you can let it go now," whispered Otis in my ear. He was the only one wearing a ski mask, to hide his appearance. Given what Smith was about to experience, it was unlikely that he would recognise any of us again, but it was not worth taking a risk with Otis.

Once I was back on my feet I could see that Smith had been hooded and the two Dobermans were all but out of it. My job now was to escort Smith to the van, strap him down and then drive to the barns. We removed Smith's bomber jacket and cap, which I handed to Otis to wear when he drove Smith's car back past the mansion.

CHAPTER TEN

WE PULLED UP ONTO THE PIECE OF LAND in front of the old Dutch barns. Reg came over to the camper, spouting various bits of Russian. I later learnt that he was saying nothing more intelligent than, "Can I have the bill please?" and "You have lovely tits." Francis responded in Russian with, "Let's get to work on this piece of shit."

Smith's body was now trembling, which was good, as gaining control through fear was key to our success. Reg stood at the end of the operating table, directly over Smith's head and spoke in English with a heavy Russian accent.

"I'm about to take off your hood. You will not speak. You will listen."

A very nervous nod of the head from Smith acknowledged the instruction. As Reg untied the hood and removed it, I took my first full look at Stephan Smith's face. The first thing that struck me was that Smith could be my son's double. It was as if Otis was lying on that table. Reg could see that I was losing my focus, and quickly jerked Smith's head back to pull me out of my distracted state. He was now squeezing Smith's cheeks so hard to make sure he had his full attention that I thought Smith's eyes were going to pop out. "You listen very carefully. You do exactly what we tell you if you do not want you and your family to die today. Understand?"

A sweat-drenched Smith nodded again.

At that point Reg gave the cue word for me to start my next task, replacing Smith's underwear with the adapted boxers. While Reg checked the restraints, I removed Smith's trainers and Francis, who had drawn the short straw, began unbuckling his trousers. Within minutes Smith was naked from the waist down. I smiled to myself when I noticed that, as the Spanish would say, 'his balls had made a visit to his throat'. Not that I was in a position to pass judgement as my privates had done exactly the same thing just twenty or so minutes ago. Once the D/D was in place Reg ran through a check to make sure everything was working. Lights flashed as he tested each button, with Francis and me taking it in turns to respond in Russian that all was working well. Smith watched everything that was going on. His eyes were constantly blinking to try to keep the sweat from forming pools in his eyes.

It was time to show Smith the movies. Reg propped up his audience of one with some pillows while Francis wiped away the sweat from Smith's face to make sure he didn't miss a single second of the action.

"You will now watch two films. Let us be very clear with you. This is what will happen to you if you don't follow our instructions." Reg switched on the DVD player and let the films roll.

I didn't have the stomach to watch the movies again, even though I had a leading role in them. I turned away to study the audience's reaction. The look of horror on Smith's face said it all. A whole new level of violence was now being played out. He'd be eating out of our hands in fear of meeting the same fate that was being delivered to those two poor victims in the films. To seal the deed, Reg offered a tempting piece of reassurance to Smith that his full cooperation would be rewarded. If he wanted to guarantee escaping this fate, Smith needed to hand over £5 million in return for his life. There was no protest from Smith. He had very quickly realised that he was in no place to argue and, for that amount of money, it was too good a bargain to turn down.

"So, you understand what will happen to you? And you are willing to cooperate?"

"Yes," assured Smith, but in a distinctly shaky voice.

"Good," said Reg. "Just remember to do what you are told and you will walk away a complete man. You understand my meaning, I'm sure."

Reg proceeded to explain to Smith in clear, simple terms what the D/D was capable of – as if the films hadn't already told Smith all he needed to know about his killer underwear! Its remote could be detonated from up to two miles away and we would be staying in very close proximity throughout the next forty-eight hours while he returned to his home. Reg pointed out that additional devices would be fitted on Smith so that we could track his every move as he gathered together the items and followed the instructions on our list. There was to be no doubt on his behalf that if he didn't stick to our orders we would finish him off, without a trace.

As Reg replaced the hood on our captive, he gave his next set of instructions. "You will now return to your car. Your dogs will still be drowsy. Be sure to tell your men that they found cocaine left on the back seat and knocked themselves out on it."

Smith did not respond so Reg repeated the whole thing in a much louder voice and with sheer aggression in his face to drive the point home. This time Smith remembered to reply.

Smith's car was parked so that when he drove off, all he would see was the rear of our 'horsebox'. Otis had left to disassemble the cordon at the south end of Wardrobe Lane. As we escorted Smith to his car, I could feel his whole body trembling. This was good; hopefully we had instilled enough fear into him to guarantee that he'd do the sensible thing and follow our orders to the letter.

Reg was already in position, monitoring the tracking devices on Smith. Francis needed to change and more importantly check out the dog bite that the Dogo had delivered. It had managed to rip his jacket and shirt and some blood had seeped through. At least if the first-aid kit couldn't sort it out, Otis would be back shortly to deal with anything more serious. Reg reported that, so far, it looked as though Smith was being a good boy and following our orders. As soon as he arrived at his mansion, he bellowed for two of his men and gave them a bollocking for spilling coke in his car. One was then given the task of taking the dogs back to the kennels, and the other was despatched on cleaning duties to make the car spotless.

Conscious that I needed to concentrate now on driving us back to the campsite, Reg said he'd let us know if anything important came up and put his headset on so that I wouldn't be distracted. I secretly wondered if he was protecting me from hearing Smith vent his anger on the rest of the family. Back at the campsite, we made a quick check to see if there were any new campers or unexpected visitors, but the torrential rain had put most people off venturing out that day. The dart guns, spare darts and handgun were placed into the false bottom of the safety tool box in the back of the Transit for good measure. We put some dust sheets, tins of paint and a variety of brushes on top to ensure that if the vehicle was inspected at customs or broken into the tools would be enough to satisfy curiosity. Given the security at the campsite the chances of anyone trying to steal the Transit were remote, but we still demobilised it for good measure once we had parked it up. The plan was that Francis would return in ten days' time to dispose of the equipment, load up his personal possessions and return to Spain, all above board.

Stephan Smith was halfway round the M25 when we pulled out of the campsite. Reg was driving, so I took the opportunity to take a look at the recordings of what Smith had been up to back at home. As I suspected, it didn't make for pleasant viewing. From the moment he stepped inside the house, Stephan Smith let rip at any and everyone who came into his patch. "Keep the fuck away from me, slag," he yelled at a young girl trying to cling on to his arm and welcome him home. She was definitely either stoned or drunk because she ignored his words and started to stroke his face. Suddenly Smith's fist could be seen flying towards her face and the girl fell to the floor. He kicked her body out of his path and carried on through the house. At that point, I turned off. I was happy to leave the monitoring to Reg, who clearly had the stronger stomach.

We were now heading for our next hotspot – the Channel Tunnel. Making contact with Smith by phone, we ordered him to buy an open return ticket with his credit card. He had done this with no problem. The next hurdle was Customs – English and French. Stephan Smith's reputation preceded him, and in the past he was always being pulled over for stop and searches.

However, after one incident with a frustrated officer who had been determined to find something on Smith, the faithful Buxton had stepped in and pursued a claim of harassment. The court had no choice but to judge in his favour. Since then, officers had received instructions that searches were not to be carried out on Smith unless there was very good reason to do so. We instructed Smith that if questioned, he was to state that he was travelling on business to meet with his bank advisers in Amsterdam and Switzerland and viewing a property development in Spain. As luck would have it, Smith was stopped, but he delivered his alibi word-perfectly. There can be no doubt that Customs suspected they were being sold a lie, but they knew he wasn't stupid enough to be carrying anything with him so it wasn't worth taking the risk of carrying out a fruitless search.

Once he was safely across the border, Smith duly headed for the designated service area. The exchange with Otis was going to take place in the largely deserted parking area for campers and caravans. At best, only a handful of vehicles would be parked there at this time of year. Never once questioning our orders, Smith turned off his engine and lights and waited for us to meet up with him, supposedly before continuing the journey to Amsterdam. How disappointed was he going to be when he woke up to find himself in a cell and the victim of a sophisticated charade! Francis and Reg walked over to Smith's car and got inside to carry out a little health check which, they insisted, was in his best interests. With the presence of the D/D always at the front of his mind, Smith agreed to have his blood pressure taken. Francis carried out the procedure and reported that the reading was far too high for Smith's own safety. Reg told Smith that he was making himself too nervous and needed a little something to bring it under control, otherwise he was likely to have a heart attack at the wheel. Smith meekly took the sedative, unaware that it was strong enough to send him into a deep sleep.

While I waited with Otis for the instruction to collect the other two, something prompted me to tell him, for once, just how proud I was of him. The difficult part was looking him in the face as I said it, because he was now transformed into Stephan Smith, complete with a number-two haircut and two fake gold teeth. Francis had done a good job of making Otis look like our number-one target. The phone rang for me to come round to Smith's car. I didn't even have time to wish Otis good luck, which played on my mind as we drove out of the services and back onto the motorway. Francis had already set to work on Smith, in his new guise as a worse-for-wear Spurs fan still drowning his sorrows over last week's game. Mid-journey, Reg and I changed places. He'd managed to nap for a couple of hours and was ready to take the wheel while I grabbed forty winks myself.

* * *

The gentle slowing down over a series of sleeping policemen woke me up. I couldn't believe that I had slept solidly for four hours. The lights from the garage forecourt lit up the inside of the van. It was a nasty shock to look across into the face of the still-sleeping Smith. Reg appeared and beckoned for me to get out.

"Good timing," he said, once I was out of Smith's earshot. "We're just over a hundred miles from the Spanish border. You ready to swap now?" We had already decided that I would be at the wheel and Reg would be in the passenger seat for the France/Spain border. Reg's command of French and Spanish was a hundred times better than mine, so if anything needed explaining it made sense for him to speak.

The forecourt was empty and only the sound of Francis refuelling the tank could be heard. The smell of coffee suddenly reached my nostrils.

"The cafeteria was closed I'm afraid, so it's machine coffee. They're only small, so I got two each."

Reg handed me two cups and I knocked them back, one after the other. Now all I needed was to stretch my legs for a couple of minutes and I'd be back in the land of the living.

"Next stop, Spain," declared Reg. It was a nice thought, but we'd got to get over the border first!

It was six-thirty when we reached the foothills of the Pyrenees. Daybreak was nearly upon us and the traffic had started to build up, which was in our favour. The sound of a can of lager being opened set my tastebuds tingling.

"Sorry gents, but you won't be able to join me," said Francis smugly. He was getting himself and the back of the van to look like a piss-up had taken place. He had filled two carrier bags and the waste bin with the empty cans that we'd been saving since we set off for England last week. Francis had poured some cheap whisky over Smith's crotch and down the Tottenham t-shirt he was wearing. For good measure, he soaked two tea towels in beer and left them in the sink to fill the already fetid air in the back of the van.

As we approached the border, the motorway widened out to

four lanes. The two outer ones were packed with trucks crawling nose-to-nose up the steep pass. Reg took out our passports and held them out ready for inspection. I went with the flow of the traffic and slowly French passport control came into view. The thirty or so cars in front of me didn't seem to be stopping. As we got closer, I could see the reason why. The cabin wasn't manned!

"One down, one to go," declared Reg.

We moved slowly into the no-mans land between France and Spain. Most of the cars ahead of us were being waved through, with only the odd one being stopped for closer inspection. Finally our turn came. "Passport," demanded the officer.

Reg handed the four passports over and the officer shuffled them in his hands for a few moments. Looking across at me, he asked in Spanish why I was wearing a Barcelona shirt. I always called it my lucky shirt but it didn't feel as though it was living up to its name today. Reg quickly jumped in with our well-rehearsed story and invited the officer to peek at our hungover Spurs fans, still wallowing in their misery. The sorry sight of Francis and Smith dozing in the back earned a laugh from the passport officer as he handed us back our passports.

"We've done it," I thought to myself as we moved away from passport control. I spoke too soon. A few yards ahead of us, another officer was flagging us to pull over. I duly obliged and move out of the line of traffic.

"Stay calm, Paul," advised Reg. "Francis? You on standby?" he asked.

"Fine, Reg," came the reply. If anything went wrong now, he'd need to give Smith a lethal injection. That was what we all agreed. If a hotspot blew our plans sky-high, Smith would be executed and efforts wouldn't have been in vain.

As the officer walked towards us, he was joined by two younger colleagues. My heart leapt into my mouth.

"Buenos dias," the officer greeted me. I returned the greeting then indicated in my best sign language that he'd be better off talking to Reg. It quickly became clear that it wasn't our passenger they wanted to know more about, but the football match. As passionate Barcelona supporters, the men couldn't resist the opportunity to get a first-hand account of the match plus the chance to gloat at some real Spurs supporters!

Asking our permission he stepped inside the van to admire our display of football paraphernalia spread over the seats and table. He turned his attention to Francis, and pointed out to him that it was going to be embarrassing for Tottenham in a few weeks' time. Reg had to translate. "It isn't over till the fat lady sings," replied Francis in English. The officer looked to Reg for a translation, who explained that Francis meant that it's not over till the final whistle. The officer laughed and shook his head. "I heard that Tottenham supporters were mad, you crazy," he replied, then he looked down at Smith and said "Crazy? They got that right!"

Still chuckling as he rejoined his colleagues, the officer gestured for us to move off. I didn't need a second invitation. As we drove away from the border, the welcome sound of lager cans being opened reached my ears.

"There you go." Francis handed both of us a can of lager. I checked in the rear-view mirror for any police escorts before taking a swig.

"What shall we toast to?"

"How about Barcelona's most loyal supporter?"

"That'll do me, Reg," I said, and downed a third of my can.

Reg picked up his Land Rover at the restaurant and drove in front of us as a precaution. If there were any problems going up the track to his farm, we could transfer Smith over. Passing the Romma's without stopping was virtually impossible. Besides they'd want to let us know that the farm and the dogs had been in safe hands while we'd been away. It was usually Hossa who would go up and let the dogs out in the morning and lock up the house at night. As expected, as soon as we stopped, the whole family descended on us with a basket of fresh supplies. The Romma's were staunch Barcelona supporters so we offered them a bag full of souvenirs in return. It didn't take long for someone to notice who they presumed to be Otis asleep in the back. Grandfather Romma had always boasted that he'd never visited a doctor in his life. Since meeting Otis and learning that he was a doctor, though, he had started to become a hypochondriac, constantly seeking diagnosis for his latest ailment. We took it as a good omen that the wily grandfather had mistaken Smith for Otis. When the Romma's heard that Otis had got drunk last night and was still sleeping it off, they laughed at the fact that a doctor had made himself ill.

Both Shake and Spear greeted us as we drove into the courtyard. Reg and Francis opened the barn door and I drove straight in. The doors were pulled firmly shut behind me. While they carried out a quick check of the property to make sure we were alone, I moved the dozen or so bales of straw that covered the trap door. On their return Francis and I carried Smith to the hatch and lowered him down. I estimated Smith weighed between fourteen and fifteen stone, which as a dead weight took all our strength to control. Personally I would have been willing to drop him head-first down the steps, as would Francis I suspect, but we both knew that we now had serious merchandise on our hands.

The sound of a sliding bolt, the turn of a key, the slam of the door. For hundreds of years prisoners knew these sounds meant one thing, they were captive. This was something we knew Smith feared more than anything. He would cheat us out of hearing his despair today, but knowing what lay in store for him, we could live with that.

CHAPTER ELEVEN

ALISON AND I HAD KNOWN EACH OTHER FOR THIRTY-TWO YEARS, and in all that time I had never once deceived or betrayed her. It was the furthest thing from my mind and I can honestly say I would have been ashamed of lying to her. Call it old-fashioned values, but that's what I believe in. If you love and respect somebody, you don't cheat on them.

That said, for the past few months, I had conveniently abandoned my long-held morals. My simple justification was that telling Alison what we were doing and bringing Stephan Smith back into our lives would have been the cruellest thing I could do to her. Neither Alison nor anyone else must know what we were doing. Avenging the rape of our daughter was to stay secret between me and my three partners all the way to the grave.

"I will have to let you go away more often. What's come over you?" she said, playfully fending off my passionate kisses.

I joked that it was my newfound passion for Tottenham to blame. The truth was that the last four months of tension of waiting to kidnap Smith had been lifted. During that time I'm ashamed to say our lovemaking had been done more out of duty. This morning was a different matter. I wanted to show Alison that my love for her was still as strong as it was on the day we got married.

I arrived back at Reg's just after ten; both Reg and Francis were sitting at the large oak table, their eyes fixed on the monitoring screens. I could tell in an instant that something was not quite right. I peered at screen four which showed the cell interior. From the picture, I couldn't make out whether or not Smith was asleep on his bed.

"Everything ok?" I asked.

"Perfect." Reg spoke first, pushing the ultimatum book across the table to Francis.

"So?" I pulled up a seat and waited for an explanation.

"It makes for very interesting reading." Reg rose and took the empty coffee pot and two mugs from the table. I thought he was going to ask if I wanted coffee, which I did, but instead he said, "Your stand on legalising drugs might take a bit of a u-turn after you've read what Mr Smith has to say." Reg went off to make a fresh pot of coffee. I looked down at the book and then at Francis.

"So, did he fill it in?" I asked.

"Yes, no problem. He did almost exactly what we asked."

"So why...?"

Before I could finish my sentence, Francis interrupted me. "If you read the answers he has given you'll see what Reg means."

Now they were both at it – talking in riddles! "How did Smith act when he saw the book?"

"As predicted. He knew that he was in a no-win situation and got down to work."

"Good job too," I said, relieved to hear of another victory for HOLI. "Reg's plan is on track then?"

"You'd better read Smith's answers first, Paul."

I did as I was told. The first thing that stood out from the page was Smith's handwriting. It was neat and tidy, nothing like the illiterate scrawl I was expecting, and the grammar was word perfect. It took just five minutes to read his answers to our questions. However, it was going to take a hell of a lot longer to come to terms with what they revealed. Reg had always maintained that once Smith was incarcerated it would be easy to extract the information we needed. What didn't make sense to me now was why he would give it in such detail. From his written 'confession' Smith was not only placing a noose around his own neck but bringing the rest of his family down with him too.

Reg returned carrying a tray of coffee, cups, glasses and his trademark bottle of brandy. Without asking, he placed a brandy glass in front of me and poured a large one. "I expect you could do with that?"

I wasn't about to disagree and gratefully took a large sip of it. Reg walked over to the fireplace to pick up a different book which had been placed near to the fire to dry out. The book was warped and its corners curled up, but it was still legible. "Perhaps you'd like to read his first attempt too," suggested Reg. The answers Smith had given in this book could not have been more different from the ones I had just read:

1. How many people have you, your family or associates killed? Give details.

   We have never killed any fucking one unless they fucking asked for it. I can't give fucking details if I've never fucking killed anyone.

Smith had already contradicted himself by saying he never killed anyone because he'd already admitted he had only killed people who asked for it, silly bastard. I continued reading.

2. Name your suppliers.

   We don't do drugs so we don't need fucking suppliers.

3. How do your drugs get into the country?

   Ask them your fucking self.

4. Name your main dealers and how you supply to them.

   We don't supply drugs so I can't give you any fucking names.

5. Name each of your UK and offshore accounts.

   All the details of my banking are held with my solicitor and cannot be accessed unless I'm there in person.

"So what made him change his point of view?" I asked. "Or should I just be relieved that he started to see straight in the end?"

"To be honest, I was surprised that Smith didn't kick off from the moment he came round. Instead, he just looked up at the camera, then went over to the table and opened a can of drink. The amount of medication that we'd pumped into him must have made him pretty dehydrated. My guess is that knowing he wasn't about to get his bollocks blown off must have given him a bit of confidence, hence the cocky answers first time around. How we got hold of the truth is all on film. Take a look for yourself."

I thought that what I was about to witness would give me a lot of pleasure, but I also wished that every person that Smith had ever terrorised could also be present. It took just one flick of a switch to release the torrent of ice-cold water from the ceiling valve. As it cascaded over Smith's head, his face twisted and contorted as he screamed, begged and pleaded for salvation. The sound of water gushing in to the cell from the ceiling almost drowned out the sound of Smith's voice as he pleaded for his life, "Turn it off you bastards. I'll talk" he vowed, "but only if you stop the fucking water NOW."

It sounded promising but we weren't going to let Smith sham his way out of the cell so we let the water reach chest height before closing off the valve. As the water subsided through the drain in the cell floor, our drowned rat prepared to make his full confession.

I was impressed at my own handiwork. The cell had stood up to the job – everything had worked like clockwork. "So, what's our next move?"

"That's where we'd got to when you arrived, Paul. We decided to dissect each answer one by one and after that, to revise our plan accordingly."

I agreed, so Reg read out the first question. "How many people have you and your family or associates killed?"

"Well, he certainly covered his own arse here."

Smith answered that he never killed anyone, his brother Rick and friends always dealt with that side of things. He claimed he had no idea how many people, but guessed it must be between fifteen and twenty altogether. As for disposing of them, their bodies were taken to Small Lake Cemetery.

"What's important here is the cemetery," said Reg. "It turns out that it used to be one of the largest cemeteries in the country, but no-one has been buried there for decades. The only visitors today are sixteen protected species of wildlife. The cemetery was closed to the public and designated a conservation area. What better place to dispose of a few bodies and all within easy reach of Smith's mansion."

"So let's move on to the next three questions that focus on his drugs business. It's not the details of his dealers, useful as they'll be to Malt, that are really valuable here, but how the Smiths move their goods around that really spills the beans. Smith has given us way more information than we dared hope for."

It seemed that Smith had created the perfect illegal distribution centre with a safety net. He stated that only ten percent of the vehicles that entered or left his property had drugs on board. The rest were transported via a toilet situated in an unused box room at the top of the house. Anything flushed down there ended up in a ditch a quarter of a mile away hidden in a private wood. The pipework was undetectable because it ran parallel to other pipes from the mobile homes used by the kennel staff as well as the waste and storm pipes from the kennel block.

It was clever stuff, I had to admit. The smugness in his tone and evident pride in his description of the set up convinced me that Smith was telling the truth.

"Now we know where he stashes his drugs, we have just got to make sure there are enough on the premises when Malt makes his next raid," said Reg.

After the high of Smith's revelations, his final response brought us back down to earth: *"The information about my accounts is impossible for me to give you. We have devised a safety net that is infallible. There are two code books, you now have mine in your possession. The second book is held in our personal vault in the Osswagen bank in Amsterdam. The vault is only accessible by fingertip recognition. One print must be mine, the other two must belong to any combination of the named family or friends whose fingerprints have been registered. There's also a six-digit combination lock, which I can give you, but without the fingerprints, the number is pointless. The truth is that unless I am there in person you cannot open the vault."*

It seemed we had come up against a brick wall. For half an hour or so we tossed around ideas about how to get the other side of it. I even suggested cutting off Smith's middle finger and giving it to Otis, but there was the small problem of putting it back on Smith afterwards to avoid awkward questions.

"But what would happen if Stephan Smith died for whatever reason? Surely the vault wouldn't stay closed then?"

"Nice thinking, Paul." There was only one man who could answer that question and Reg was straight on the case. He moved over to the control desk and spoke into the microphone linked to Smith's cell.

"Stand up and look up at the camera." Smith did this without question. "You have told us that a finger print is needed from three people to open your vault and one of them must be yours. So what would happen in the event of your death? Does the vault remain locked indefinitely?"

"Antje and Klaas are both directors of the bank. Both of their right-hand middle fingers can activate the electronic vault sensors to open my vault. It would still need two registered members to be there plus Buxton, my solicitor, because he has power of attorney. The bottom line is that you or I cannot get to a penny until I'm released. I am willing to make a deal with you. Let me make some phone calls and I can have £50 million put into any account anywhere in any currency you want."

I gasped at his ability to deal in such massive sums with relative ease. What was this man's real wealth?

"We will speak to you again shortly," replied Reg.

"Well gentleman, any ideas?" Francis got up from the table

and walked down to the fire. He stared at the flames for a few minutes, as if the answer lay there, and then returned to the table and started jotting down notes on paper. We had to wait a good quarter of an hour before he would share his idea with us.

"Paul, you might not like what I am about to suggest, but hear me out. For the record, Reg has no idea what I am about to say." The one thing the four of us will have to decide is if we have already got enough on the Smiths to have them put away."

"It's all circumstantial evidence until those bodies are found and Malt locates a ditch full of coke," pointed out Reg. "I think we should keep digging to get as much evidence as we can against them. That second code book holds a lot of answers."

"I agree with you, Reg."

It seemed that both Francis and Reg wanted to get their hands on the second code book. We had photocopied every page of Smith's own book and let Otis keep the original. Most of it was just rows of numbers, which without the other book meant nothing.

"So what's this plan, Francis?"

"The way I see it is that we need three sets of fingerprints to get into that vault. Altogether, we have a choice of sixteen people whose prints would do the job. I reckon that from the list of names Smith has given us, Clark, Amtree, Schaaf or Kuiper are our targets."

"If you think about it, Clark and Amtree have spent the least time with Smith. Both of them have been working for less than four years and in that time and, if my memory serves me right, they've both done eighteen months inside for GBH. For my plan to work, Otis, in the role of Stephan, will meet Clark and Amtree twice."

Francis could instantly see I was uneasy with this plan. "Otis would never get away with that. His impersonation of Smith was purely meant for the cameras and people who didn't know him, not work associates. It's too risky," I protested.

"I know where you're coming from, Paul, but hear me out," Francis continued. "We always maintained that four principal factors would determine the success of operation HOLI. Splitting apart the family loyalties to each other was one, relieving them of their wealth was the second. Bringing them all to justice was third, and the hope that the law when it finally caught up with them would pass sentences that fitted their crimes was our fourth. We could accept Smith's multi-million pound offer and send him back on Monday to face the music and Malt, but for two things. The answer to question three and how much Smith is actually worth. When I first read what Smith had written down about how their drugs get into the country, it proved to me what Reg has always maintained. Trying to hold back the tide of drugs coming onto our streets is impossible. Like it or not, these drug barons have come up with an ingenious solution for getting their drugs under the net."

Francis read out Smith's answer as a reminder: *"I'm not sure how they do it, but all the drugs come in via containers from the Far East. They come as granite or marble. The supplier has a way of compacting the stuff so tight that it forms into heavy rocks. These are cut into slabs, pillars and tiles and when they arrive in England they are taken to a trade warehouse that I own under an alias. The goods are stocked under a specific product range, each with their own, unique descriptor. So when someone orders, for example 'Heritage marble slabs' there can be no confusing the product with any of the real marble or granite goods in stock. The warehousemen have no idea what they are shifting into the lorries. Most drops are made to large properties in the country or out-of-town storage, all safehouses that I have set up. There the goods will stay until I give the go-ahead for them to be moved. From there, the goods are picked up on an as-needed basis and taken to a workshop where we break up the slabs using cutting machinery. Within two hours we'll have the drugs in our hands. As for our supplier, Mr R, I've never met him. I make payments via my offshore accounts every two months. Again, the details for these transactions are held in the bank vault in Amsterdam."*

"So the problem we have is that if we don't take Mr R out of the equation, he'll be free to start up all over again. By catching the Smiths, we only damage the flow of drugs on to our streets; to stem the source we need to target the people bringing the stuff into the country."

"The best you can hope for is to channel the supply, not stop it," pointed out Francis, and that means making them legal."

"You're right," I declared. Suddenly I was agreeing to something that I long considered unthinkable – the legalisation of drugs.

"The bottom line is if that we need the second code book. I believe some of those numbers are parts of postcodes and relate to the properties where Smith picks up the marble."

"Well, there is only one way to find out." Reg resumed his interrogation of Smith, who obligingly gave us the much-needed information.

We learnt that the properties where the goods were stored were managed by a letting agency, who acted for an offshore company which in turn belonged to R.L.M.C., the company owned by Mr R. There were just over two thousand properties on the agency's books. We had estimated that the codebook held about sixty postcodes, so these must be the main properties that Smith used for storage. Not only was Mr R using his property as a cover to bring drugs into the country, he was using them to launder money. Buying to let and paying taxes on ill-gotten gains is one sure way of increasing your money legitimately. If we could prove that just one of his properties had, at some time, received a delivery of granite or marble, then Malt could call the bloodhounds in to that address. This was precisely the kind of operation that the Proceeds of Crime Act had been set up to tackle. Getting hold of those postcodes would leave Mr R with some explaining to do.

"Well, let's hear the plan and then decide," suggested Reg. I agreed, but my one thought was that we had come through the worst and detection of HOLI was unlikely, so why jeopardise what we had got for what could be gained.

Francis proceeded to explain his plan. "We get Smith to instruct Rick to contact Mr R and to allow us to pick up 330 kilos of marble so we can have it crushed and bagged up on money day. Stephan will also tell his brother that one-third is to be left at their place. The other two-thirds will be split and placed in safe houses. Smith will also inform his brother that he wants Clark and Amtree to fly out to Amsterdam for Thursday so that they can be at the bank the next day to open the vault. Stephan and Rick Smith hold a certain amount of respect for Clark and Amtree who could be trusted to carry out any amount of dirty work in return for financial reward. Reg and I will fly out a day earlier and arrange for two high-class prostitutes to meet us the following night at the hotel where Otis is staying.

On the Thursday, Otis, as Stephan, will ring Clark and Amtree to say he's running late having spent the last couple of hours in A&E getting his hand fixed after trapping it in a taxi door. He tells them to go on the town for a couple of hours before meeting him at eight for dinner. When we arrive at the hotel bar, Otis will be on the phone pretending to be in a heated discussion. Reg and I, with assumed identities, will introduce ourselves to the party. Otis will ask Reg to come with him, explaining that they'll be back shortly."

"That will be my cue to suggest that we retire to Stephan's room to relax with the girls, who have been briefed beforehand to give their very best performances. Once we're up in the hotel room, I'll get everyone on the vodka – Clark and Amtree are bound to be well oiled by this time, after going out on the town earlier on – and slip some Rohypnol into their drinks. This will knock them both out by the time Reg returns with Otis sporting a plaster cast on this hand. Otis, in the typical manner of Stephan, will dismiss the two ladies leaving us to sort out the men."

"On Friday morning at ten o'clock we will arrive at the Osswagen bank and inform reception that we need to speak to Kuiper or Schaaf. I'm guessing that the amount of business done by Smith and Mr R with the bank will put them at our beck and call. Clark and Amtree will arrive looking and feeling like shit. Otis will tell them to get their fingerprints taken and then return to their beds until they look and feel better. This will be the only exchange of speech between them. As for Schaaf and Kuiper, it will be obvious why they have been summoned when they see

Stephan's hand. With three sets of fingerprints and the ten-digit number we should have no trouble getting into our safe." Francis smiled with satisfaction at his ingenuity.

"Far be it for me to say that it's not a good plan, Francis, but it looks like one hell of a gamble."

Reg was one hundred per cent right. It was a great plan but its success came down to one thing – whether Otis could pull it off. His appearance as Smith wasn't the problem, it was if Clark or Amtree got close enough to start up a conversation. Otis and Francis had worked hard over the past three months trying to perfect and change his speech and mannerisms to match Smith's, and with the little footage they had to work with they had done well.

"The decision as to whether we go with this plan has to be unanimous." I thanked Reg for that. "So perhaps the first thing we should do is ring Otis to let him know."

Francis picked up the mobile and moved over to one of the settees to tell Otis what we had discussed. Reg and I decided that it was time to draft the letter to Malt. To give himself enough time to put the wheels in motion, Malt would need to have the letter in his hands by the following day.

"He's in," reported Francis. Knowing my son's taste for derring-do, I might have guessed what his decision would be. "His one concern is how well do Schaaf and Kuiper know Smith? Perhaps we could check with the real Mr Smith when we speak to him next."

"Well, you know my decision." Francis sat back down at the table and Reg looked across at me. "Do you know, Paul, if we carry this off and even though we will never receive recognition, it might be the turning point for a review of drugs legislation, once they appreciate that these drug cartels are serious businesses, milking the very core of our society." Reg paused, and then declared, "I'm in."

"Good, now let's find out how well Schaaf and Kuiper know Smith."

Reg was at the microphone, preparing to interrogate Smith once more.

"Smith, we require answers to the following questions. If you cooperate fully you will be released in five days."

Smith had reached boiling point. The frustration was clearly visible on his face, but he knew that complying with our orders was going to be the only way to safeguard him leaving the cell alive.

Reg proceeded to give Smith a set of very precise instructions about ordering in the drugs through his brother, Rick, and arranging for Clark and Amtree to fly out to Amsterdam. He also instructed him to make sure that the family would be around to give his new Russian partner a very warm welcome when he came to collect his goods from the Smith's place.

Smith didn't say a word. He just stared up at the camera, fists clenched, awaiting the next instruction. For his whole life he had ruled the roost; for him this was humiliation at its worst.

"My first question is how well do you know Kornelis van der Schaaf and Hindricus Kuiper?"

Smith was taken aback by this. "Why?"

"My question is can they be trusted?"

"My question is why?"

"Because when you are in our business, banks that can be

trusted are hard to find."

This seemed to satisfy Smith. "They earn enough money out of me to be trustworthy." This didn't tell us anymore about how well these men knew each other, but we needed Schaaf and Kuiper for the ten-digit number to the vault.

Reg decided to see how far he could push Smith. "Give me those ten digits or we'll cut off your finger." Smith looked panicky. "But I can't remember ten numbers," he protested.

"You have one minute to bloody well try." Having made the threat, Reg would have to follow it through if Smith didn't cooperate, so we were more than relieved when we saw our prisoner move over to the table and start writing something down. Smith held the piece of paper up to the camera for Reg to read out the numbers.

"And you confirm that these are the correct numbers?"

"Yes," Smith said resignedly.

We had to assume that Smith was telling the truth. If he wasn't then we were going to be in trouble. The sound of the cabinet sliding through into Smith's cell made him turn away from the camera. Seeing the mobile phone must have given him hope. He read through the list of instructions supplied and then rang the number. We listened in at the control desk to make sure that the conversation didn't stray from our instructions.

It was Rick who picked up the phone at the other end, and immediately demanded to know where Smith was. Stephan cut him dead and told him to listen to his instructions. Rick kept quiet until Stephan told him about storing a third of the coke at mansion.

"But you can't bring any more to the house," said Rick, we're already holding two hundred and fifty kilos."

"For fuck's sake, why?" asked Stephan, genuinely shocked.

"You know why, we haven't done a milk round for nearly two weeks. Nothing's moving."

"Listen, we will move everything on Monday, just make sure everyone is there including Buxton. This Russian guy is expecting a warm welcome."

"I hope you know what you're doing. Oh and by the way, the next time you decide to knock a bird dead in this house, remember to clear up your own dirty work." With that parting shot, Rick rang off.

"Oh hell, that poor girl on the video. He really did kill her." I could see that the others were still reeling from the shock. We sat in silence for a few minutes to let the news sink in, before taking up where we'd left up with renewed determination to topple Smith from his throne.

"So what's a 'milk round' all about?" I asked.

"No idea," Reg replied, "but I know a man who does." He turned on the microphone and summoned Smith to the camera.

Smith dragged himself off the bed and stared up at the camera, but this time he looked angry.

"What now?"

"You followed instructions, but what are the implications of 'the milk round'? Can you explain?"

"No I fucking can't. I'm not answering any more of your fucking questions and I want some decent fucking food."

Reg turned to Francis and me. "Seventeen minutes seems to be an appropriate number, gentleman," and with that he flicked the switch. For the second time today cold water flooded into the cell. It took mere seconds before Smith was pleading for his life in return for the information we needed. Reg kept the water flowing for the full seventeen minutes. None of us took pleasure from watching the process, but we knew it was necessary and thoroughly deserved.

While the heaters dried out the cell, Smith was given fresh clothes. He then quietly delivered us chapter and verse on the milk round. According to Smith, his family had every major town in the South of England covered. As suspected, the night that Francis had followed the two Smith brothers and their sidekicks into town, a drugs drop (or milk round) was carried out in the Chevy. It was one of a fleet of such vehicles (or milk floats) that had been customised to provide the necessary storage recesses to carry the drugs, and flash fittings to disguise them while in transit. There was even an emergency flushing system that disposed of the drugs down a storm drain if the milk round ever encountered any police.

"You've got to hand it to them, it's a good operation," said Francis. "They ought to be on Dragon's Den!" "Malt will be chomping at the bit for this information," said Reg, "I think it's time we wrote him a letter, gents." It took just under an hour to produce the following:

For the attention of former Chief Superintendent Jamie Russell 'Malt'

For three decades Stephan Smith and his family have avoided capture and conviction for a catalogue of crimes including murder and rape, and miscellaneous anti-social offences. Their devious and smug attitude which is propped up by their wealth has long been a source of great frustration for our national police force. The cheque in front of you now shows my support and the authenticity of what I am about to tell you such that you will be able to use it as evidence and proof in a court of law. No doubt, your superiors, the judge and the jury will ask for the source of your information. Your answer is simple. This information comes from a concerned member of the public who wishes to remain anonymous. We will never have to meet; all contact will be made by phone. I will use the codename HOLI and I suggest you adopt the name FOSS. You are welcome to change that, but in due course you will see why the name might suit.

Operation FOSS will be a costly exercise, and with the three previous failed raids, your superiors might be reluctant to proceed without good information. I'm prepared to give you a second financial injection within the next couple of days to ensure that you have no problem in convincing your superiors that operation FOSS must go ahead.

My first set of evidence is that by his own count, Stephan Smith, members of his family and his henchmen have between them murdered up to fifteen people in the past three years. The latest victim was just three days ago. A girl about seventeen was murdered by Stephan Smith's own hand. For footage of this incident please see the enclosed DVD. Her body, along with Smith's other victims, is buried at Small Lake Cemetery, probably the side that backs on to the private woodland which is owned by Smith's parent company. I leave you to decide how best to follow up the grim task of recovering the bodies.

In the past, raids on Smith's property have been unsuccessful. The reason for this is that a sewage system has been put in place and connected to a separate ditch, or foss, about a quarter of a mile away. Any illegal substances on the property would be immediately 'flushed' down the system via a toilet on the top floor and effectively removed from the premises. Detection of this pipework would have been impossible because of the depth it was buried.

For operation FOSS to be a success, you must be prepared to raid Smith's mansion at Wardrobe Lane on the fifth of March at two-thirty pm, when you will find every member of the family and gang gathered there to meet an important new contact for their trade. You can also expect to find about three hundred and sixty kilos of coke on site. Shortly you will receive a detailed list of other properties that have been used as safehouses for storing the goods. I suggest that raids on a selected shortlist will prove just as fruitful for you.

I appreciate the mammoth task that you and your officers will need to undertake to have the necessary preparations in place within such a short space of time. I assure you that the end reward of seeing Smith and his family behind bars will be well worth your efforts.

I will contact you this evening at five o'clock to update you on the latest developments.

Good luck, Malt,

Holi

Francis volunteered to arrange the delivery of the letter. He thought it best to let one of his 'women' do the job, to eliminate any chance of HOLI being identified. Meanwhile, Reg needed to go into town, which left me to look after Smith. We had installed a freezer and microwave outside the cell to reduce the risk of being seen carrying food over to the barn. I wasn't looking forward to being the babysitter but had decided that adopting a cold, regimental approach would help ease the burden: a bowl of cereal for breakfast at nine, a sandwich for lunch at one and a ready meal for supper at seven. Fetching and carrying his meals was galling enough, but having to listen to Smith's whining voice whenever he knew someone was outside the cell was the worst. Still, I was going to have to get used to it because I was going to be his prison guard while Reg and Francis were over in Amsterdam. I'd have to tell Alison that I'd offered to look after Shake following a minor op at the vets, but I knew she wouldn't mind. "Anything for Reg," she'd say.

CHAPTER TWELVE

REG AND FRANCIS ARRIVED AT THEIR HOTEL IN AMSTERDAM late on Wednesday evening. The next morning they met for breakfast and gave me a call to check that everything was in order. I confirmed that all was well and wished them luck in their mission. Their first port of call was a bookshop on the other side of town. It gave Reg a chance to meet up with an old acquaintance but, more importantly, it served as an alibi for their trip.

Their next stop was a furriers. To make a convincing pair of Russian aristocrats, they would need to have the right wardrobe and that meant investing in real fur coats, the ultimate status symbol in Russia. Francis picked out a three-quarter length white mink coat with matching Cossack hat while Reg opted for a modest fur stole with the head of the fur's original owner still attached.

Back at the hotel, Reg concentrated on finding two classy ladies-of-the-night to help out with the next evening's entertainment. A few discreet enquiries yielded a phone number that offered precisely the kind of services that they had in mind. Once done, all that remained was to set about transforming themselves. Changing Reg's appearance to make him look like a hard-faced mafia boss took quite a bit of work. Designer stubble hardened the contours of his face, and brown contact lenses hid those sexy blue eyes that Alison so admired. A token gold tooth and a stylish black suit did the trick. Meanwhile Francis had become a real Russian beauty, the type that only James Bond ever gets to meet. He had chosen a long shiny black wig that flowed from under the white Cossack hat and over-the-knee boots to draw attention to her perfectly formed thighs. The aim was to keep the male attention on Francis and steer any close scrutiny away from Otis. As they left the hotel lobby to get a taxi, several men swivelled their heads to take a second look at the hot vixen who had just passed them by. It looked like Francis had picked the right woman for the job, yet again.

Reg and Francis met up with Otis at a bar and restaurant almost opposite the Osswagen bank. Otis had come straight from the hospital where he had spent three hours having two of his fingers reset. He had decided to inflict the injury on himself so that his dressings and splint would be authentic enough to convince both Clark and Amtree as well as the bankers. Francis and Reg admired his commitment and quick-thinking solution. They ran over their arrangements for the evening to check that everyone knew their parts, then headed off to the hotel to meet their visitors. As soon as they spotted Clark and Amtree in the hotel bar, it was clear that the call girls, Laima and Aija, had done their job well. The men were nicely relaxed and well oiled.

Seeing their boss on approach to the bar, both men started waving wildly, calling him over to join them. Reg promptly pushed the send button on his phone to ring Smith's mobile which was on maximum volume to ensure that Clark and Amtree heard it ring. Otis answered instantly, adopting the loud and commanding manner of Smith. He littered his sentences with Smith's favourite expletives and slowly developed the fake conversation into a full-blown argument. At the same time, he gestured to Reg and Francis to join the others and introduce themselves, inviting them to enjoy the bottle of Russian vodka that he'd ordered for their table. At the sight of their guests, both men eagerly leant forward to make their acquaintance with Reg's partner, Nadja, much to the disgust of their escorts. Smith was still on the phone, arguing furiously with Mr Nobody, but made certain to keep his back to the group at all times.

As the group sat round the table Amtree asked Aleksei (Reg's alias) what exactly Smith had done to his hand. Reg recounted the story of how a taxi driver eager to pick up his next fare had started to drive off before Stephan was fully out of the car. As the car pulled away, the taxi door had slammed back and trapped his hand, breaking two fingers in the process. It didn't take a lot of effort to convince the two drunken idiots that he was telling the truth. His phone call complete, Smith walked over to Aleksei and told him they needed to go. Amtree and Clark instinctively offered to go with them, but Smith just shook his head and turned towards the lobby. "No need. We'll be back later" came the blunt reply.

As Reg and Otis made their way out of the hotel bar to another one a couple of streets away, Francis suggested to the rest of the group that they made a move upstairs. Once inside the room, Clark sat down at the table and prepared five lines of coke. Aija sat with him and Laima headed for the en-suite. The door linking the lounge and the bedroom was left open and Francis could see clearly in to the room. Laima had been in the en suite since we arrived and Amtree was getting agitated; this was good for Francis as it gave him a clear run to drop the sedatives into the men's shots without being seen. The tablet would take thirty seconds to knock them out so it was imperative they both took them at the same time.

Francis knew his number-one task that night was to put Clark and Amtree out of action, but then something happened that put the whole plan into jeopardy. Francis had placed all five shot glasses and the vodka on the tray, taking a sip from one of the glasses so as to leave a trace of lipstick to indicate which one was his. Clark was now rolling a one-hundred-Euro note ready for a big snort. Francis had planned to bring the tray over to the table, hand the shots out and make a toast when everyone was together. However a loud bang followed by a scream scuppered his plans. Laima was being dragged with her knickers round her ankles from the en-suite by an impatient Amtree who had just kicked the door in.

Not only for the sake of the plan but for the frightened Laima, Francis needed to act quickly. He was going to have to take a chance and give the men their shots separately. Walking over to Clark and Aija he handed them a shot glass each and said "How you say in England? Bottoms up."

All three downed the shots in one. Francis then refilled his own glass and the other glass which he had dropped the tablet into and made his way to the bedroom. Amtree had already lashed out at Laima with his belt, and her back glowed red with the sting of the strike. Now he was adding a series of punches to her petite face and demanding that she spread her legs. His sheer pleasure from such sick behaviour was clearly visible from his skywards facing hard-on. Francis drew close to him and whispered, "I hope it'll be my turn later, big boy."

Amtree couldn't believe his luck. He snatched up the shot from the tray and knocked it back to celebrate his lucky night.

"Dream on, mate," thought Francis. He quickly passed the empty tray to Laima, indicating that she was to use it as her exit pass to escape from the bedroom. The offer was accepted gratefully and the girl was out of the door in a moment.

A thud on the lounge floor told him that Clark had succumbed to the sedative. "Now for Amtree to follow suit," muttered Francis, as he invited the man to lie back on the bed and propped a cushion under his head as if he really cared about the evil brute. Within seconds, his eyes were shut and he was out for the count. Francis went back in the lounge, where the girls were tending to Laima's wounds and nursing their shaken nerves. He thanked the girls for their generous services beyond the call of duty and handed them a large bonus to compensate for the outrageous behaviour of Amtree.

Once the girls had left the flat, Francis set about moving Clark to the bedroom, placing him alongside Amtree with their arms entwined in a warm embrace — a satisfying payback for these two sadistic animals and raging homophobes. He then cleaned up, flushing away any remaining drugs and tidying up the damaged en-suite door as best he could. The last thing the operation needed at this point was any police involved and it would only take a chamber maid to set that in motion.

* * *

There would be nowhere to run if Clark or Amtree got the slightest suspicion that their boss was not who they thought he was. We had to rely on them having the mother of all hangovers such that thinking only made their heads hurt more. It had been arranged that all four men would meet in the bank at ten-thirty. Otis had thoughtfully arranged an early alarm call from the hotel reception to give Amtree and Clark enough time to drag themselves out of bed and make the meeting on time.

Reg later described the massive open-plan lobby of the bank as an impregnable showpiece, carefully guarded with pairs of security men at each and every door and boasting at its centre a stunning life-size bronze statue of a figure driving six oxen. There was no telling what Smith's vault was going to reveal. In this respect, operation HOLI was on the brink of its biggest gamble ever. Never ones to let things worry them, the team decided to savour the glory of their surroundings while the going held good. After letting a receptionist know they had arrived, Otis, Reg and Francis stopped to admire the bronze statue. Otis stepped into character and starting talking loudly to his friends. He looked completely out of place in such sophisticated surroundings.

It was Kuiper who emerged from the lift. They recognised him from the staff profile on Osswagen's website. Kuiper greeted Smith without a hint of suspicion and introduced himself to Aleksei and Nadja. Both men talked for a few minutes about how Smith had come to sustain his injuries but like all bank managers, Kuiper's time and courtesy only extended to what could be gained financially. Luckily he was willing to invest a little extra time in making the acquaintance of Nadja, who had clearly attracted his eye. They chatted easily for five minutes or so, until Clark and Amtree shuffled in looking like they'd been to Hell and back. As Nadja flirted with Kuiper, the party made its way down the stairs to the vaults. Otis reminded himself that Smith mustn't comment on the impressive arrangement of strongrooms, as he would have seen all this before. He left all the talking to Aleksei and Nadja who had been given permission to accompany Smith because they had expressed an interest in leasing their own vault at the bank.

Kuiper stopped outside a vault bearing the number sixteen on its door. He stepped up to the sensor pad and placed his forefinger on it. After a few seconds, a red confirmation message of 'Accepted' flashed up on the display. Kuiper stepped back and gestured for Clark and Amtree to take their turn. Clark went first, clearly eager to get the business over and done with so he could get back to his bed. Both men's prints had their acceptance confirmed. Now it was Smith's turn to enter the ten-digit combination, the final 'key' needed to open the vault door. Had the real Smith delivered the true code or had he just been lying through his back teeth? They were about to find out.

Carefully Otis typed each of the well-rehearsed numbers into the keypad. As he pressed the last digit he could hear his own heartbeat. The 'Accepted' message appeared instantly. The number had been right. Smith had told the truth for once in his life! With their access to the vaults assured, the team now needed to get rid of Clark and Amtree as quickly as possible. Anyone who has ever suffered a severe hangover will know that being told to go and sleep it off are magic words. Smith dismissed the men, telling them to get some rest and he would see them back at the mansion on Monday. They didn't need to be told twice, and were gone in seconds!

A smoked-glass door was all that separated my partners

from the second code book. Before Kuiper made his exit he shook hands with each of them, emphasising that he looked forward to seeing them again in the near future. Both guards had now taken position either side of the vault. This was normal procedure once a vault door was open. No-one liked to fall at the last hurdle; it adds insult to injury. The team were facing a large safe at the end of the vault that Smith had conveniently forgotten to mention. A six-digit number was required to open it. It was at that point I received a call telling me to use whatever means were at my disposal to extract the numbers from Smith, and fast.

From the security monitor I could see that Smith was lying on his bed. Grabbing the microphone, I spoke to him. "Stephan Smith. There is a second safe in the vault at Osswagen Bank. What are the six digits needed to open it?"

Glaring up at the camera, Smith replied, "I don't fucking know." I suppose I expected that, but it left only one course of action open. I had no sooner pressed the button for the cell to start flooding when the sound of frantic tapping suddenly filled the room. I froze at the sound of this unscheduled interruption and, for a split second, I thought saw the entire HOLI operation unravel before my eyes. Bracing myself for the worst, I slowly turned towards the window with what I hoped would pass as a casual glance but I wasn't confident that it would win me any Oscars!

I strained to focus on the figures at the window and as the shapes became clearer I couldn't believe my eyes! Peering back at me through the smeary glass were five faces from the Romma family, pleading to be given shelter from the torrential rain. Oh Christ! What could I do but let them in? I switched off the surveillance camera which was now showing Smith screaming obscenities at the screen, then made a quick final check around the room to make sure it was clear of anything that might arouse suspicion. With a deep breath and forced cheery smile, I opened the door to let the bedraggled neighbours inside. Hastily I offered them something to drink – always a welcome distraction! As I filled each of their glasses with a generous slug of wine, they explained that a male boar had gone on the rampage and old man Romma had shot it but only wounded it. Of course he blamed everyone else but himself for his bad shooting.

While I struggled to make sympathetic and concerned noises in the right places, divine intervention in the form of a strong ray of sunlight shot through the lounge window and came to my rescue. For in less than a minute the freak downpour had stopped and bright blue sky appeared once more. I pushed the front door open to feel the heat of the sun and watched it going to work on everything that had been soaked. Vapour rose like clouds of soft smoke, even the Romma's, who had seen all kinds of weather up here, were impressed. I did the rounds with the brandy once more, hinting that it was one for the road. It did the trick. A few minutes later I watched the five men walk towards the farm entrance shouting for their four dogs. The firm voice of their master tore them away from trying to find out what was going on in the barn.

"Bloody hell, even Reg couldn't have planned a luckier escape than that," I muttered to myself as I waited for my heart to return to its normal pace. As soon as the men were out of view I cautiously returned to the security camera to see how Smith was coping. The water had risen so high he was standing on his bed, pleading for the water to stop. I switched off the valve and opened the drain to release the water. In a way the Romma's had done me a favour. When I repeated the question to Smith, he recited the six-digit number without argument. I rang straight through to Reg and stayed on the line long enough to hear the word 'Bingo'. I rang off leaving my partners to get on with the job in hand while I returned to Smith. Anyone who did not know what Smith was capable of would have felt pity for him. I was reminded of the words of Judge DK Turner which Reg had read to me once from an old law book. They made perfect sense to me.

"There can never be an excuse for a person who continually commits crime, be it serious or petty, because the individuals who persist in these illegal acts have had the time to reflect, change, stop and consider. They continue because they want to continue and only death or incarceration will stop them. Then so be it."

* * *

Back in the vault, Otis, Reg and Francis were uncovering a wealth of treasures. Apart from the code book, there was a bundle of forged passports, driving licences and ID cards; deeds to properties in South America and Africa; and a hefty stack of crisp, new Euro notes. Working their way along the units of shelving, there were gold bars, trays of jewellery, paintings and antiques. "Look at that," said Reg. "There's even a stash of saffron. It's the most expensive spice in the world. The amount they've got here would make a pension on its own."

At the far end of the vault was a small office comprising a desk, two chairs and a couple of laptops. Reg took a seat and started up the computer. Within minutes he was setting up money transfers from Smith's offshore accounts. Once the transactions were complete, Reg declared it was time to go. It was bank policy that a member of the bank's security team should be present on closing the vault. Reg carried out the code book and Otis took one final photo of the vault and its contents to provide proof of what lay inside. They waited patiently while the guard carried out the procedure for sealing the vault, then returned to the lobby where the day's adventure had started with a none-too-promising outlook.

The feeling of relief and reward was shared by all three of them as they walked out into the cold air. They were brimming with pride at what they had just achieved. Money might not bring you health and happiness but in reality you still need to have it.

When Reg and Francis arrived in Amsterdam, as a precaution they had parked the hire car a mile away from the hotel in an underground car park. It was the only connection to them as they had used false names and paid cash at the hotel. It was only a ten-minute walk away from Osswagen so the three men walked together before going their separate ways. Reg and Francis would return to Spain and Otis was to head to Geneva for a couple of days before flying to Malaga. Only then would operation HOLI be reunited again.

* * *

Early on the fifth of March we drove to the appointed service station fifteen miles north of Malaga to rendezvous with Otis and make the swap. In the past I had spent up to twelve months without seeing him, but the past eight days had seemed like a lifetime. I was determined to tell him how proud I was of his achievements and how much I loved him. How and when I would do this I didn't yet know, as I still felt uncomfortable when it came to showing my emotions.

Otis had hired a Range Rover from an executive car hire firm using Smith's passport and ID card as proof of identification. We had arranged to meet in the overflow car park where it was less likely to be busy. Otis had parked as far as possible from the entrance and we parked alongside to shield the Range Rover from anyone coming into the car park. Otis looked physically exhausted, which was not surprising given that both he and Francis had averaged about four hours of sleep a day over the past week or so. Otis would have been caught on probably half a dozen different cameras that morning in the hotel, so having Smith in the same clothes was paramount. Otis only had to get Smith into jeans, trainers and jacket; we had already placed him in his own boxer shorts, t-shirt and socks. In the unlikely event that Smith reported his kidnapping to police, we took the precaution of brushing and steaming these items of clothing before dressing him. As Otis removed the gold paint from his tooth – the last reminder of his life as Smith, Reg and I placed the still-unconscious Smith in the passenger seat of the Range Rover. Now all we were waiting for was Jeanette.

Driving Smith the three miles to the airport to catch his flight was too dicey for us to carry out, so Francis conjured up a sophisticated hippy from his wardrobe to do the job instead. Jeanette now hopped into the driver's seat of the Range Rover and started up the engine. Taking the camper was too risky so it had to be done this way. If Jeanette was pulled over by the police, she would tell them that she was taking Smith to the hospital because he had fallen unconscious. If they insisted on escorting her there, then would she would have to give them the slip at the hospital once Smith had been dealt with. Reg had given Smith a shot of adrenaline to start bringing him round, and there were two cups of black coffee in the cup holder to help accelerate the process. On the journey, Smith started to become more aware of his surroundings, and by the time they had reached the drop-off point, he was fully conscious. Jeanette signalled for him to get out of the car, handing him a mobile phone that had been sitting on the dashboard. At that moment the phone rang, which was Jeanette's cue to drive off.

"Smith, are you listening?," asked Reg in a heavy Russian accent. "You will find your ticket to London in your jacket pocket. Hand the paperwork and keys back to the hire firm and don't forget your suitcase." Before Smith could respond, the voice on the phone issued more instructions. "We will meet 2.30pm British time at your home. Make sure you're there."

* * *

At about the same time that day, Malt was addressing an assembly of some five hundred police officers. There was an air of excitement as Malt laid out in careful detail his plans for the raid on Smith's property. There was nothing worse for a bobby than to see a criminal not pay for his crime. This time they were going to be fourth time lucky!

CHAPTER THIRTEEN

"Chief inspector russell?"

"Yes."

"It's HOLI. Stephan Smith has just gone through to the departure lounge at Malaga Airport. He will be on flight BA3288 due to land at Heathrow at twelve forty-five your time. He will take a black cab from the airport back to his home. Given no hold-ups at immigration or delays on the roads, I anticipate his arrival to be two-thirty." Francis was calling Malt from a disposable phone outside Malaga airport. "This will be our last contact with you." Francis then wished Malt 'good luck' and rang off.

Malt contacted immigration at Heathrow and advised them not to detain Smith but simply to stick to the routine procedure. We had given Smith the alibi that he'd been looking for, a property to buy in Malaga, and had put half a dozen or so glossy property brochures in his suitcase to support this. Malt still had no idea who or what HOLI was, only that they wanted to see justice done by putting Stephan Smith and his family behind bars for a very long time. It was now down to him to match their efforts and pull off the biggest sting in his lifetime.

* * *

For Stephan Smith and his family the day had arrived for them to face a daunting and inevitable question. Had Smith, a son, brother and cousin, betrayed the family and stolen from them? Reg's plan was to turn mother against son, brother against brother and all cousins and friends and business associates against each other. For this to work they would all have to believe Stephan Smith's story. Within less than four hours it would become clear if they had.

Two Dobermans and two henchmen who had worked for Smith for years stood guard behind the closed gates. Seeing Stephan get out of the taxi they quickly opened a side gate to greet him as usual. He pushed past them, shouting instructions for them to pay the driver. We had given Smith orders to instruct the family that there was to be no dealing or work carried out on that Monday. This would minimise the amount of people at Smith's mansion and help the police, who would already have thirty criminals and a pack of dangerous dogs to contend with. The block-paved drive was as long as it was wide. As Stephan Smith made the walk up to the front door, the large open space didn't feel or look right. On our instruction Smith had ordered that all cars be moved from the front of the house and garaged out of sight so as to make way for a helicopter. Again, this was simply to help the police raid by providing them with a clear access point at the front of the building.

While he waited to be let in at the front door, he noticed that unusually both Dobermans stayed at the gate rather than follow him to the house. Smith simply put it down to what had happened when they were last together. Who knows at what point the penny started to drop that he was in the middle of an irreversible sting, but being ignored by two of your most faithful dogs must have started alarm bells ringing in Smith's head. Once the security door had been opened by someone inside, Smith pushed past and headed straight for the lounge. The lounge was the hub of the mansion, where everyone met to talk, eat and drink. Four large sofas had been arranged in a square around some coffee tables. An overflowing ashtray and a half-empty bottle of vodka sat on the table nearest to Tanya, Smith's mum. From the state of her he could see that she had made an early start. David Buxton and Jack Smith sat on the sofa directly opposite the entrance to the lounge where Stephan Smith was now standing.

Jack Smith was the academic and computer wizard of the family. What he didn't know about the hi-tech world usually wasn't worth knowing. Excluding Stephan, he and Buxton took sole charge of any money transfers. Both men looked ashen. They had just broken the news to everyone gathered in the room that £1.7 billion had been transferred, lost or stolen from their offshore bank accounts. The only man who could provide an explanation for their financial dilemma had just walked into the room. There was complete silence as all eyes turned to Stephan Smith.

The series of instructions that Stephan Smith had issued to his family over the past week had tested their loyalty and patience to the limit. To hear now that there was no money was the final straw.

"What have you done with our fucking money?" Tanya Smith was the first to break the silence. "It's all fucking gone."

Stephan looked across at Buxton. "Your mother's right. The offshore accounts have been cleared out. We know that you personally authorised the transaction from the Amsterdam account. We also know that you arranged other transfers from Geneva. Look for yourself." Buxton gestured to the screen on his laptop for Smith to verify that what he was hearing was true.

"What the fuck have you done with it?" It was Rick Smith's turn to vent his anger. "And why are we holding so much stuff back?" He was referring to the millions of pounds' worth of drugs sitting in warehouses and at the mansion. "I hope you realise that if the filth raided us right now we would be wiped out. We deserve some answers, Stephan, and they'd better be good."

For once, Stephan Smith was speechless. It was suddenly dawning on him that he had been well and truly set up. Rick Smith wouldn't normally have stood up to his big brother, but with the way Stephan had ordered them about in the past week and now the loss of all their money, he had the full support of the family behind him. Stephan Smith then made one very big mistake. He started screaming back like a banshee at everyone that he had been kidnapped by a bunch of Russians and shut off from the world for the last week or so. Everything was deadly silent in the room. At that precise moment reality hit home for the Smiths.

The American penal system carried out a survey in 2006 of its one hundred thousand inmates, both men and women. Their crimes ranged from petty misdemeanours right through to the most serious crimes. Question eight on that survey asked what was the worst thing about being a criminal. The multiple choice answers were:

a) having to serve your time
b) attending court to hear your sentence
c) the first few seconds when you realise you can't avoid capture.

Of the questionnaires returned, ninety-eight per cent

ticked the box marked 'c' for this question.

The ominous sound of a caterpillar truck crashing through metal broke the silence. It took down both front gates along with the pillars and gold-plated pitbull terriers still on top. Behind the truck followed two-hundred riot police with shields and batons looking like infantry ready to go into battle. The Smith family was about to realise that the game was up.

Having done its job, the caterpillar moved aside to give the one-knock (a JCB complete with battering ram) access to the front door. Malt, along with his officers, knew from previous experience the strength of the Smiths' heavily reinforced front door, hence the modified JCB to take on the job. Once the battering ram had gone through the door a lever inside the cab would release four posts which would spring out like an umbrella. The JCB would then reverse at speed hopefully bringing the door with it. There was a possibility that the framework and half a tonne of masonry might want to join it. Malt had inadvertently 'forgotten' to mention this and the umpteen other things that Health and Safety might have taken a dim view of. A clerical error had also informed Health and Safety that Operation Foss would be taking place on the sixth of March, a day later. Malt would be reprimanded and dragged over the coals for this error weeks later over a celebratory lunch with some senior officers and presented with a crate of the finest malt whisky.

The sound of the battering ram taking out the front door raised the battle cry of the troops, as eighty or so men dressed in full riot gear rushed in. Malt had waited three decades for this moment, during which time he had had to witness and endure the family's constant flouting of the law. Clouds of dust still hung in the hall as Malt made his way through the rubble of brick and plaster to the lounge. The hit squad had carried out their orders. Every resident in that mansion was laid out on the floor, handcuffed and being searched. Malt then ordered his officers to stand everyone up in a line. At the head of the line was Buxton. Malt knew that if one person could escape it would be him, using his legal know-how to slip the net. He would quickly turn grass for several reasons but first and foremost to get witness protection. Malt had already made up his mind that if Buxton cooperated fully, and that included providing his fingerprint to open the vault in Amsterdam, he and his family would get a completely new identity. At this point no-one knew how much money and property belonged to the Smiths or their suppliers. Reg had done a quick evaluation based on their monies, property, stock and money owed, and estimated that it could well exceed £2 billion. Buxton would sing like a bird; he knew that Smith and his cronies were dead men walking.

Malt continued down the line, stopping to take a good look at each face. Often he was showered with abuse and spat at, but he showed no emotion. As Malt came to the end of the row, only the chorus of helicopter blades, barking dogs and urgent voices could be heard outside. Malt turned to his sergeant and said, "Nick 'em."

Malt later described the next forty-eight hours as the best and worst times in his career. The satisfaction of finding the horde of drugs and impounding them was overshadowed by the discovery of the mass grave of victims found at Small Lake Cemetery. The forensic team had enough evidence to prove that each of those poor souls had at some point spent time at Smith's mansion. After that, it didn't take long for the family's loyalties to fall apart as they realised what was coming to them. They all knew their lives in or out of prison would depend on police protection. Operation HOLI had achieved its final objective.

* * *

We had used the Barcelona-Malaga game as the alibi for our journey, so as planned we headed for the ground, parked up and grabbed forty winks. We were all absolutely whacked out and it wasn't until the car park started to fill up that the hustle and bustle finally woke us up. Watching Barcelona completely annihilate Malaga was painful because in all probability we might have to witness our beloved Tottenham face the same ordeal. We left just before the first half, with Barcelona playing an excellent game and three goals up. I took the first shift at the wheel with Francis alongside me, while Reg and Otis searched the internet for news. It didn't come as a surprise to see Stephan Smith's face appear on screen, followed by scenes from the raid and an aerial view of Small Lake Cemetery.

I was worried about the impact on Alison and Charlotte of seeing Stephan Smith splashed over the television and newspapers, but there was nothing I could do about it. As we drove through the night, Francis and I chatted casually and we moved on to the subject of Charlotte. He wanted to put my mind at rest that she would be able to handle the sudden reappearance of Stephan Smith. He confided that on a recent evening out together, Charlotte had started to talk to him about her ordeal. Throughout she had spoken about it in the past tense and made it very clear that she had moved on from that period in her life. Francis said that she firmly believed that people like the Smiths of this world get their comeuppance one day, but in the meantime she was not going to let his actions dictate and determine the course of her life. I was so relieved to hear that Charlotte had really moved on – she had taken hold of her life and claimed it back for herself. I thanked Francis not only for sharing the information but for being the person that made this change in my daughter's life possible.

We arrived back at Reg's just before nine and headed for home straightaway. The others knew I was anxious to be with Alison in case she took the breaking news badly. The Smiths' arrest and the discovery of the bodies at Small Lake Cemetery took precedence over the rest of the world's news. The can of worms we had opened was now on view for the world to see. We had played our point and should have been taking it easy, but fear can taunt you in different ways. The fear of Stephan Smith and his family coming back into Alison's life after what it did to her last time was something I couldn't bear. The extent of the media coverage now and for the next few months was going to be impossible for her to avoid. I looked to the advice of my grandad who would often say, "If you don't know what to do, do nothing because doing nothing still leaves you with an option to do something." It sounded like a good idea.

As I pulled into the yard, several chickens were scratching about at the front of the house in the spring morning sun. I took a few minutes after getting out of the Land Rover to take stock of how lucky we were to live in such a lovely place. Alison's car wasn't about. She had probably called in for coffee with Maria at the bakery after dropping Charlotte off to catch the college bus. After making myself a large mug of coffee, I went back outside and sat down on the bench under the kitchen window. I bent down to pat my old dog. You could always tell where the warmest part of the house was by where you found him stretched out.

The sound of a car engine snapped me out of my reverie. It was Alison. Loving and living with your best friend, you can tell in an instant when something isn't quite right; she was still sat in the car and I felt sure that my worst fears were about to be confirmed. In one hand she carried a small cardboard box of pastries. In the other hand she carried a handful of Spanish newspapers.

"Tell me we couldn't have stopped this," she said, stepping out of the car.

I took the box of pastries and papers from her, and asked her to come into the kitchen. It was ironic seeing Stephan Smith's face staring up at me from the table where the papers lay. Alison was now shaking uncontrollably, repeatedly asking, "Does Charlotte know? Does Charlotte know?" I needed to do something quickly if I wanted to avoid her falling victim to another mental breakdown. The thought of my wife slipping back there was more than I could bear. I had to get through to her in the shortest possible time that everything was going to be okay. Grabbing both shoulders and looking her straight in the eye, I told her, "Charlotte's okay. She can handle it. She opened up to Francis and has moved on from that part of her life. And to prove it, it seems that those two are..." I stopped for a second, not knowing whether Alison would want to hear this or not.

"I know," she said smiling. I held her tightly and kissed her cheek. "Tell me we did the right thing, Paul. We couldn't have stopped all those people being killed, could we?"

"Listen, Alison, to what I am about to tell you." I needed to be firm for both our sakes because this shadow of guilt needed to be removed from our lives.

What Alison wanted to know was whether any of Smith's victims would still have been alive if I had taken a different course of action at the time of Charlotte's rape. The truth is I knew Smith's resources, and if they thought there was a chance of going down they would have been hot on our heels. Could we have won the day? I don't know, but I knew that Smith had a get-out clause and jumping bail was his last resort. It was there for the taking. If I had learnt one thing about the Smiths it was that there was a continual flouting of law and they must have had a back-up plan or some sort of insurance. Alison listened to my careful explanation and nodded in agreement. We held hands across the table for a while. How much I wanted to tell her what I had done to avenge what she and Charlotte had gone through. I knew that the person I would share the rest of my life with was the one person that I couldn't tell.

***

On a sombre Monday morning at the beginning of August, Stephan Smith along with his pair of brothers, two cousins, mother, stepfather and four members of what the press had dubbed "the cemetery gang," stood in a converted number-one courtroom at the Old Bailey. Tension and hatred against the judicial system as well as each other was running high among the accused, so they had been segregated from the public and divided between three cells: one housed Stephan Smith, one held the rest of the family, and the third contained the cemetery gang. Since being charged five months ago, they had not seen or spoken to one other. True to form, each had strived to save his own neck by grassing on the other, spilling the exact details, names and places of crimes that created a disturbing montage of two decades of vicious and cold-blooded activity. The loyalty and trust that the Smith family and their associates supposedly held in such high regard had crumbled into a pile of sand, turning brother against brother, Mother against son and friend against friend.

HOLI had proved that apart from Smith's Eurolottery win all of his other monies and assets were the direct proceeds of crime. Naturally there was a public outcry when he was allowed to keep his £56 million on the understanding that he paid all court costs. This gave Stephan Smith the opportunity to buy back the loyalty of his family and friends by paying for their legal teams, but as the full extent of their predicament revealed itself, hatred quickly corroded any remaining warmth they felt towards him.

How the tables had turned for Smith, stripped of all credibility and respect that he had built up during his bullyboy reign. Smith's family and business associates turned against him in full force and he knew that there was a price on his head. His ranting and raving in court bordered on hysteria; he was clearly angry and bitter that he had endured kidnap and torture for the sake of friends and family who had now thrown any gratitude back in his face. They had lived off his 'earnings' and reputation for years but now when it counted most they had turned against him. It was this betrayal that Stephan Smith simply could not handle.

The case took three long weeks as the catalogue of crimes revealed itself and the evidence produced by HOLI sealed the fate of the accused. The jury of five women and seven men was directed by the judge that if it could agree that each one of the eleven accused were responsible for at least one murder he would be satisfied. This relieved the jurors of the onerous task of having to consider each individual case which would literally have taken years to complete. For five days, the members of HOLI together with families of those who had been victims of Stephan Smith, his family and/or the cemetery gang, were on tenterhooks awaiting the jury's decision. They need not have worried as the verdict was unanimous on all counts: Guilty. The courtroom erupted with screams and sobs from the public gallery and triumphant cheers from some of the victim's families. As the accused were dragged away from court by their guards, they turned their eyes towards their fallen leader and screamed abuse, each and every one swearing to get revenge on Stephan Smith.

* * *

"Happy birthday to you, happy birthday to you, happy birthday dear Grandad, happy birthday to you."

There were many reasons why Operation HOLI was a success; seeing those two children holding that birthday cake and singing to Reg must rate among them. It was almost seven years to the day since we heard that Stephan Smith, his family members and henchman had been told that they would spend the rest of their lives behind bars. For us and our extended family, life had gone in a totally different direction.

Otis had made the decision to pour his skills and the money into opening drug rehabilitation units across Europe. He had started a drugs education and awareness programme to be run through schools. Both of these were registered charities and received substantial support and funding from several governments. The two children who had just sung to Reg were testimony to that. Five years ago, on the steps of one of the first rehabilitation centres in Manchester, he had come across a woman, weighing less than seven stone, who had been badly beaten. With her were two dirty, undernourished toddlers. Her name was Elizabeth Anne Challenger. For Reg, being reunited with his daughter and discovering that he had two grandchildren had sealed the aching gap in his life. Elizabeth, David and Jane made regular visits during the year to spend precious time with Reg. He valued their company and cherished these special times like a good harvest of grapes that were bottled until the next visit.

For Charlotte and Francis, the past seven years had been hard work bringing up three children, all boys, and building their successful business. Theirs was what marriage was all about, pulling together. Seeing their three boys playing in the pool with Reg's grandchildren and Otis's son Daniel was proof that Charlotte and Francis had made it work. As for Otis, he had met Carol through his work. She had been on his staff and they seemed to gel from the outset, both in their work and private life.

Alison and I could not have been happier. However, if I could have a magic wand I would ask for one more thing. I would like governments throughout the world to look at their drugs policies and consider legalising some drugs. I never thought I would agree with Reg, Francis and Otis on this issue but what I had seen and learnt through Operation HOLI made me believe that we don't have an option. Even with all the good work Otis has achieved, he still maintains that if you had a child taking drugs you would rather them go via legitimate routes instead of using some street-corner dealer.

As for the Smith's and their goons, the promise of hell visiting them every day became reality. They spend their days banged up in their cells for their own protection, apart from Smith, who after less than a year, was transferred to Broadmoor where he asked for special protection. As for Buxton, he disappeared off the face of the earth.

It is not often that the four of us have the opportunity to get together up at Reg's these days, but when we do we keep to a tradition of having a drink together at the bar in the barn which now houses a swimming pool, but which was originally Smith's cell. Today was no different, and as we watched and chatted and as our families laughed and played, and while the smell of pine burning for the Rommas' barbecue filled the air, we raised our glasses and quietly raised a toast to Operation HOLI.

Friends are like stars
you dont always see them
but you know they are there